Figuring Out
Frances

GINA WILLNER-PARDO

Clarion Books
NEW YORK

Clarion Books
a Houghton Mifflin Company imprint
215 Park Avenue South, New York, NY 10003
Copyright © 1999 by Gina Willner-Pardo

The type was set in 13.5-point Apollo MT.

Printed in the USA.

Library of Congress Cataloging-in-Publication Data

Willner-Pardo, Gina.
    Figuring out Frances / by Gina Willner-Pardo.
        p.   cm.
    Summary: Ten-year-old Abigail's neighbor Travis, her best friend
although he is at a different school, upsets her when he transfers to her
school, ignores her, and laughs at her grandmother's Alzheimer's along
with his new friends.
    ISBN 0-395-91510-4
    [1. Best friends—Fiction. 2. Friendship—Fiction. 3. Schools—Fiction.
4. Grandmothers—Fiction. 5. Alzheimer's disease—Fiction.] I. Title.
PZ7.W683675Fi   1999   98-50082
[Fic]—dc21   CIP
                                                          AC

                QBP   10 9 8 7 6 5 4 3 2 1

For Jim, who's better at talking

One

"I can't imagine the boys I know in suits," I said.

"Not suits, exactly. Uniforms," Travis said. "At my school we all wear uniforms."

"I don't know if I'd like that," I said, feeling the hammock sway beneath me. "Everyone looking the same. Like little grownups."

"You don't have to figure out what to wear every day," Travis said. "That's the part I like."

"I guess I see," I said. I wanted to like what Travis liked. We'd known each other since he was three and I was two. That's eight years. Best friends should always like the same stuff.

We didn't go to the same school, because most of the time Travis lived in San Francisco with his dad. He took a city bus to his school, which was all boys. He had to pray every morning. He'd told me that sometimes when he was supposed to be praying he couldn't help thinking about whether the 49ers were going to win that weekend or what the nuns would say if he burped as loudly as he could. Mostly, though, he tried to think about God and doing good deeds.

Every other weekend Travis lived next door to me with his mom and her new husband, Donald. Actually, Mrs. Blankenship had been married to Donald for almost three years. He wasn't so new anymore. He and Mrs. Blankenship were guidance counselors at the high school. They talked to kids about their problems and how they shouldn't smoke or use drugs and what college they should go to. Travis said they got to hear all kinds of juicy stuff. They weren't allowed to tell him any of it, though.

"I like Earl Cronkite Elementary School," I said. "We get pizza every Friday, and Mrs. Swift lets us take turns making morning announcements on the intercom. And we can wear jeans and sneakers, as long as they don't have holes."

"We have fish sticks on Friday," Travis said.

"And I like having boys and girls at school." Even Joe Cristophe, who shoved his whole fist in his mouth at the second-grade talent show. Even Philip Cassavetes, who eats rocks. "School wouldn't be school without the boys."

Travis grabbed the edges of the hammock and tipped his body from side to side. The hammock began to rock again. I held on to my end of it and grinned as Travis rocked us higher and higher. It was one of our games: seeing who'd hold out the longest.

Finally Travis said, "OK, Abigail, stop. I'm all dizzy." We stopped tipping and the hammock slowed. I liked that Travis didn't mind being the first to give up.

"I wouldn't mind going to school with girls," he said. "And I'd love to wear jeans to school. Those gray pants itch."

"Don't they even let you take the jacket off when it's hot?"

"Just for a couple of weeks in September," Travis said.

"Marlene says she'd go on strike if she had to wear a uniform," I said.

"You can't go on strike against a *school*."

"She says wearing a uniform would stifle her individuality."

"Girls in general are OK," Travis said, "but I don't see what's so great about Marlene."

"I've known her since kindergarten, first of all. Which makes her my second-oldest friend, after you. And she's the best in the whole school at tetherball, and she can sing 'Over the Rainbow' with wiggles in her voice, like a grownup."

"Her teeth are too big," Travis said.

"And she takes tennis lessons, and tap dancing, and soccer," I said. "And her father says when she's thirteen, he's going to buy her a horse."

My mother was always saying that I should have Marlene over a lot because she was a good influence. What I liked about Marlene, though, was that she liked to do things like burp underwater and open her mouth wide when it was full of creamed corn. Things no one would expect, and my mother would definitely hate.

"Anyway, what about *your* friends?" I said, leaning forward and grabbing the bag of cheese curls off his lap. "I think Marshall is an idiot."

"You've never even met him. Even *laid eyes* on him."

"I've heard about him. I know everything I need to know. What kind of kid tries to get good enough for football by running into walls?" I stuffed a handful of cheese curls into my mouth. "And Wizard. *Wizard*—what kind of name is that?"

"He knows everything. He's good at everything." Travis grabbed the cheese curls back. "Plus his real name is Winston."

"I guess Wizard's better than Winston," I said. I stuck my foot out of the hammock again and touched it to the deck. "We should have nicknames. For each other."

"Yeah." Travis half sat up. A couple of cheese curls fell from his chest into his lap. "Picking a nickname yourself is better than getting stuck with one that someone else made up."

"What do you want to be called?"

"Hmm." Travis screwed up his face all funny, thinking. His straight black hair was mashed into the back of his head from lying in the hammock. His cheeks were two red dots from the heat. "How about Speedy?"

"You *are* fast," I said. "Speedy's good. Now what about me?"

I thought about how funny it was that I knew so much about Travis's life with his dad: about his school, and Marshall and Wizard, and what he thought about in chapel, and who he liked and hated. I knew everything, but none of his friends had ever seen me. Like a ghost.

"Phantom," I said. "How about Phantom?"

Travis nodded.

"Phantom is good," he said.

⭐ ⭐ ⭐

It's funny how you get to be best friends with a person. It's not like you meet someone and know instantly that that person is going to be your best friend. Sometimes it takes a while for two people to feel the same way at the same time.

That's how it was with Travis and me. For a long time we were neighborhood friends, like all the kids on the block: we rode our bikes up and down Red Valley Drive, watched TV in somebody's family room, had burping contests, looked for frogs in the creek after a heavy rain. Now, looking back, it seems as if we barely knew each other at all.

In first grade Marlene was my best friend. She didn't live in my neighborhood. At school we played hairdresser and chased boys. We thought anything was funny.

One day that year I was playing in my back yard and heard a sound over the fence. I stopped playing to listen. I'd never heard a boy crying when he hadn't just fallen off of something or crashed.

"Travis?" I called. Then I thought maybe he wouldn't want me yelling his name when he was crying, so I ran to the fence and peeked through the knothole. "Travis?"

"What?" He was sitting in the hammock with both his feet on the deck. The laces of his left sneaker were untied. He was wiping his nose on the sleeve of his gray sweater.

"What's the matter?" I asked.

Travis shook his head.

"Did you get hit?" I asked. Boys were always getting hit.

"No," Travis said. He sniffed hard. "My mom's getting married."

I didn't know what to say. I was only in first grade; I didn't understand about families being mixed up and complicated.

"Can I come over?" I asked.

Travis nodded and I boosted myself into the dogwood and over the grape-stake fence that separated our yards. I landed with a thud in the juniper bush on Travis's side. The spiny branches prickled my knees. I'd have red bumps where they touched my skin.

I went and sat across from Travis on the edge of a barrel full of dirt and zinnias. That was in the days before Travis let me sit in the hammock with him.

"At least she's not dead," I said. "My grandpa's dead."

Travis looked up from his shoes.

"That's pretty lousy," he said.

"Yeah," I said. "He coughed up blood and everything."

That's the kind of thing you say when you're six.

Travis's eyes got big.

"Wow," he said. "Did you see?"

I wanted to lie and say yes. I thought that would make me cool and make Travis like me. But even six-year-olds know you tell the truth to friends.

"No," I said.

"Well," Travis said, "I guess you're right. Getting married's not as bad as coughing up blood. And Donald's all right, except for always asking me how I'm feeling all the time."

"Does he think you're sick?"

Travis shook his head. "It's just something he always asks. He asks everybody."

"That doesn't sound so bad," I said. "My dad's always working. My mom . . ."

It was too hard to explain about my mom.

"Nobody asks me anything about how I feel," I said.

"That's funny," Travis said after a minute. "Donald asking me how I'm feeling all the time and no one ever asking you. Exactly the opposite."

It was weird, though. It felt exactly the same.

We were best friends after that. I don't think we ever said so. But I knew we were. We still rode bikes and watched TV with all the other kids on the street. But now, sometimes, we sat in the hammock and talked. Travis told me about his parents being divorced, arguing about money, slamming doors, calling names. I knew he didn't tell anybody else that stuff.

I told Travis private things, too. How my grandma couldn't always remember my name or what year it was. How my mom liked for me to wear bracelets and not get muddy. How I wished my dad was home more. At first, Travis's only being around every other weekend made it easier to tell him things: when he was away, it was as if I hadn't said a word. I knew my secrets were safe.

Soon, though, I started to miss him. Two weeks started to seem like an awful lot of time.

★ ★ ★

I wadded the cheese curls bag into a wrinkly ball and lobbed it into a giant green flowerpot that stood empty by the sliding glass door.

"I have to go," I said. "Mom's taking me school shopping."

"You're so lucky," Travis said. "I don't get new school clothes until I grow out of my old ones."

"Not clothes. Pencils and notebooks and erasers and stuff." I tipped the hammock as I stood up. "I like starting school with everything new."

"Hey," Travis said, "next time I see you, you'll be in fourth grade and I'll be in fifth."

One of the things that's the same about Travis and me is that we both have December birthdays. That means I'm one of the oldest kids in my class and Travis is one of the oldest in his.

When your best friend's a boy, you're always looking for things you have in common.

"Fifth's so old," I said.

"I know. Fourth grade's cool. We got to make models of the missions with toothpicks." Travis stood up, too. He walked over to the flowerpot and pulled the cheese curls bag out. "And dissect a cow heart and chicken bones."

"Gross." I wiped cheese curl dust on my jeans. "We get to go on the upper-class overnight in October. We get to camp out in a redwood forest. In real tents."

"I wonder if you get to see your teacher in her nightgown," Travis said.

"I never thought of that," I said. "It's hard to picture a teacher in a nightgown."

"Just think if your teacher was a nun," Travis said. He headed out toward the recycling bin. "See you in two weeks."

"Yeah. See you," I called. "Remember everything," I added, which was what I always said. Because I really liked it when he told me stuff.

Travis just waved. He never told me to remember everything. It would have sounded too much like a girl. But I know he liked it that I did.

TWO

I slammed the kitchen door. From somewhere down the hall, I heard Mom say, "Well, it's about time." I wasn't sure if she was talking to me or Grandma, but it didn't really matter. Being around my mother always made me feel as if I was fifteen minutes late.

I grabbed a glass from the cupboard and filled it with water. While I was drinking, I heard the downstairs toilet flush, and a minute later Grandma shuffled into the kitchen. Grandma has lived with us since my grandpa died. She has Alzheimer's, which is a disease that makes you forget things, like where you live and how old you are and even your own name. Grandma still knows her own name, but she calls me Frances all the time, and she doesn't remember that Dad is her own son. She calls him Stewart, which was her brother's name. No one in my family had any idea who Frances was.

"Hey, Grandma," I said, talking loudly, so she would hear. "You want to go to the drugstore with Mom and me?"

"Nope. Can't." Grandma walked slowly, pulling herself along the counter with one hand, holding her cane off the floor with the other. She looked as if she was concentrating on moving forward. "I'm waiting for a package."

Grandma was always waiting for a package. There never was one.

"You want me to get you some peppermints at the drugstore?" I asked.

Grandma didn't answer, so I waited a second, then asked again.

She shook her head.

"It's a fine day for a drive," she said.

It was like that with Grandma. Nothing she said made any sense. You got used to it, but it could drive you crazy just the same. I think that was one reason why I couldn't wait for school to start. Even the kids I hated made some kind of sense. At least they knew my name.

Mom walked into the kitchen. She is little and kind of round, with pretty brown hair that falls just below her ears and smells like pineapples. Even though she's small, she's fast and fierce looking, like Marlene's mom when she's been cut off in traffic. Only my mom looks like that all the time.

"Good Lord, Abigail, let's get a move on," she said. "It's nearly five. I want to get dinner started."

"What are we having?"

"Burritos, if we get back in time. Hurry up now. Go comb your hair."

"I don't need to. It looks fine."

Mom shot me a look that said "Do what I say," so I ran into the bathroom and grabbed a comb. I looked at myself in the mirror. Hair a little redder than my mom's, cut short and curly. Pale skin, straight, freckly nose. Skinny arms too long for the rest of me. Nice green eyes.

My hair looks fine, I thought, running the comb through it twice.

I went back to the kitchen just as Mom was saying, "You go sit in the living room, Lucille. The news is almost on."

She spoke loudly and carefully, as though Grandma was a tourist who didn't speak English and she was trying hard to be understood.

"The news! It's on in five minutes!" she yelled.

Grandma smiled and inched along the counter.

"Is that right?" she said.

Mom zipped her fanny pack shut.

"Let's go, Abigail," she said. Her mouth was a thin, straight line. I knew it made her nervous, leaving while Grandma was up and around and could get into trouble, like the times she'd fallen, or made expensive phone calls, or shouted things out the window at passing cars.

In the car Mom said, "So is Travis excited about fifth grade?"

"I guess so," I said. "Mainly about playing soccer and being a buddy to the kindergarteners."

"Fifth grade's a big year," Mom said. "I remember fifth grade. I felt grown up. All of a sudden."

"I think Travis feels the same as always," I said.

"Fifth grade was when I started caring about how I looked. And whether boys liked me. I started wearing nail polish."

I had the feeling that if Mom and I had gone to school together, we'd have had totally different friends.

"I hate the way nail polish smells," I said. "And I don't care about boys."

"Travis is a boy," Mom said.

"I know, but . . ." I sighed. I was always having to explain about Travis to Marlene. It seemed unfair that even my own mother didn't get it. "We're just friends."

"He's very handsome," Mom said.

"It's not like we *like* each other or anything," I said.

★ ★ ★

I bought pens and pencils and a shiny red notebook and graph paper and a compass for circles. And a ruler, and erasers shaped like teddy bears. And a book of dinosaur stickers, just for fun. Marlene said dinosaurs were for babies, but I didn't care.

While Mom paid for everything, I looked through movie magazines. All the boy movie stars were very handsome. Was Travis handsome? I couldn't tell. To me he just looked like Travis. My mom was always asking me who I thought was handsome. The more she asked, the more sure I was that when I finally thought of someone, I wasn't going to tell her.

Was Travis handsome? Were straight black hair and scruffed-up knees and long thin feet handsome? I tried to imagine Travis Mooney kissing some girl in a romantic movie. I almost laughed out loud.

⭐ ⭐ ⭐

When we got home, Grandma was sleeping in front of the TV and the phone was ringing. Mom crossed the kitchen toward the phone. "If this is your father saying he's late, I'm going to be really steamed," she said.

But it wasn't Dad. "For you," Mom said.

"Hey," Travis said.

"What?" I asked. Travis never called me.

"I have some news," he said mysteriously.

"What news? Good or bad?"

"I'm not sure," Travis said. "My dad got transferred to Saudi Arabia."

Mr. Mooney worked for an oil company. He was a geologist. I wasn't sure what a real geologist did, but I had a feeling it was more than just saying if a rock was igneous or sedimentary, the way we did in science lab. Mr. Mooney was nice enough, but quiet and kind of shy. He wore big black glasses that made his eyes look far away and short-sleeved shirts that showed his knobby white elbows. Sometimes I saw him dropping Travis off at his mom's on Friday afternoons. Mr. Mooney would wave at me and sort of half smile, but he never said anything. Travis never introduced us. I wondered if Travis's dad even knew who I was.

"What's 'transferred'?" I asked, even though I had a pretty good idea.

"He has to move there. For a year. It's for his research," Travis said.

My heart sank into my stomach.

"A year?" I shrieked. "A whole year?"

A year without Travis. Who would I hang around with? Who would I tell things to? Marlene was good for laughing and doing stuff with, but I couldn't imagine telling her anything important. She wasn't that kind of friend.

"But here's the thing," Travis was saying. "I can't go."

"What do you mean you can't go?"

"I can't. Dad says. He has to travel around and work nights. Dad says it would be too disruptive."

"Wow."

"Fifth grade's a pretty important year," Travis said, in a way that kind of got on my nerves.

"I don't get it," I said. "What are you supposed to do for a whole year?"

The minute I asked, I knew.

"I'm living out there," Travis said. "With Mom and Donald."

16
★

I didn't know what to say. I felt so many things at once. Relief that he wasn't going to Saudi Arabia. Happiness that I'd get to see him more. Worry that things were changing.

A lot of worry.

"You mean," I said, "you're going to my school?"

"Yeah. It's all worked out. I've got someone named Miss Cox."

"I know her from yard duty. The buttons on her shirt are always popping open." I twirled the phone cord around my index finger. "She's nice, though."

"It'll be weird calling a teacher 'Miss.' I can't even imagine it. And having girls in class." Travis was silent. "And not seeing Marshall and Wizard."

"They can visit," I said quietly.

"It'll be weird," he said again.

"The weirdest thing," I said, "will be seeing you every day. On the playground."

"Yeah. Listen, Abigail—"

"What?"

"Nothing. Just . . ." Pause. "Nothing."

"I can show you everything. The kickball field and the ball room and the drinking fountain that Ziggy Hellerman peed in in kindergarten and how you sign out if you have to go to the dentist. And where you eat lunch when it rains. And the lost and found."

Travis didn't say anything. The silence made me nervous. It made me want to keep talking.

"And I can introduce you to everyone. I know tons of kids. A couple in fifth grade, even. Lorraine Peterson took swimming lessons with me at the Community Center. Barbara Santiago was Dorothy last year in *The Wizard of Oz*."

More silence.

"It'll probably be better if I just find my own friends," he finally said.

"OK," I said.

I felt as though someone had punched me in the stomach.

★ ★ ★

The first day of school was hot and steamy. Mom wanted me to wear my new boots and a new pair of jeans, but it was too hot. I got out of it by convincing her that I'd be sweaty by ten o'clock.

"What're you doing up so early?" Grandma said as I finished the last of my cereal.

"It's the first day of school," I said. I was surprised. Usually Grandma couldn't tell whether it was early or late.

"Is that right?" Grandma poured herself a cup of coffee and sat down at the table. "What are you taking?"

"The same as last year. Reading and math and social studies and science. In science we get to make volcanoes with baking soda and vinegar."

"I thought you were a real biology whiz," Grandma said.

"I don't think you can take biology in fourth grade," I said.

"Don't let them push you around," Grandma said.

"They're not pushing me around, Grandma," I said. "I'm not even sure what biology is."

"Be true to yourself, Frances," Grandma said. "Don't take no for an answer."

"I won't, Grandma," I said. I'd learned not to argue. It was easier just to pretend to be Frances. Whoever she was.

Dad came into the kitchen.

"Hey, sweetie. Hey, Mom," he said.

"What are you doing here?" I asked.

"I live here," Dad said.

"No, I mean, it's after eight o'clock." Usually my dad left for work at six-thirty, before I even got up.

"I thought I'd hang around today. Maybe drive you to school." He leaned over and planted a kiss on the top of my head. "Big day today. First day of fourth grade."

"Mom says fifth grade's when you start to feel grown up."

"In my book, fourth grade is a much bigger deal than fifth grade." Dad washed an apple in the sink and took a bite. "Fourth grade is huge. I mean, before fourth grade, you're in, what? *Third?*" Dad waved his hand, as if third grade was a fly that had to be shooed away. "And after fourth grade, there's only fifth. Sixth. Seventh.

Just more of the same." He shook his head. "Fourth grade is very, very big."

"Oh, Dad," I said, but I laughed anyway.

"I've been telling Frances not to get talked out of biology," Grandma said.

"Good advice, Mom," Dad said. He checked his watch. "Come on, Abigail. How about a ride?"

I swallowed the last of my cereal.

"Sorry, Dad. I'm walking today. With Travis." When Dad looked puzzled, I added, "Travis Mooney, from next door."

"Oh, yeah. Your mom said something about him living there full time now." Dad looked disappointed, and for a second I was tempted to forget about walking. I never got to spend time alone with Dad. Being a lawyer took up most of his day.

"How about we pick Travis up on our way?" Dad asked.

"Thanks anyway." Friends and dads just didn't mix. Everybody just sat there, not talking and feeling embarrassed. "Maybe if you come home early tonight, I can tell you about everything."

"I'd like that, sweetie." Dad took another bite of apple. "I'll shoot for six. How's that?"

"OK." I knew he'd never make it. "Bye, Dad. Bye, Grandma."

Grandma waved her coffee spoon at me.

"You remember what I told you," she said.

From somewhere upstairs Mom yelled, "Abigail! Get a move on!"

I grabbed my lunch from the counter and my

backpack from the kitchen shelves and ran out into the sweltering September morning. It was the kind of day when you wanted to be underwater as long as the sun was out. Or sitting perfectly still under a big tree, or lying in a motel room, like the one we stayed in at the Grand Canyon, with the curtains drawn and the air conditioner on high. School was the last place you wanted to be.

Even if you were starting fourth grade, which, maybe, no matter what your mom said, was a big deal. Even if you were walking there with Travis Mooney.

★
21
★

Three

The only thing was, Travis Mooney wasn't home.

"He left about fifteen minutes ago," Mrs. Blankenship said at the door.

"He did?" That jerk, I thought. I was sure he'd want to walk with me, especially since it was the first day.

"I think he wanted to get to school a little early," Mrs. Blankenship said. "You know, check things out. Get the lay of the land."

I nodded. I felt silly. Mrs. Blankenship was looking at me funny.

"You understand, don't you, Abigail? Travis just needed to handle the first day on his own."

"If I were new, I think I'd want a friend around," I couldn't help saying.

"Being new is pretty tough," Mrs. Blankenship said. "Different people have different strategies."

Strategies was one of Mrs. Blankenship's guidance-counselor words.

"Well, I'd better hurry," I said, backing down the front steps.

"I offered to drive him. He didn't even want *me* around," Mrs. Blankenship said.

I could tell she was trying to be helpful. But what I wanted to say was, You're his mother. Of course he didn't want you around.

I'm his best friend.

★ ★ ★

Earl Cronkite Elementary School's playground was full of kids. Most of them were wearing new clothes: boots and sweaters and leggings and overalls. By lunchtime they'd have heat stroke. I felt lucky in my shorts and T-shirt.

Marlene was standing under the big maple tree in the center of the playground. She was tanned from swim team and spending August water-skiing at her aunt's house on Lake Tahoe. She was holding her long, frizzy black hair off her neck and blowing upward at her sweaty forehead.

"Why is it always so hot on the first day of school?" she asked. "Why is it so hot before the first bell?"

"I heard that you get sent home with a note if you don't wear deodorant," I said.

"They can't make me wear deodorant," Marlene said. "LeeAnn says it's against the law to make someone wear deodorant if she doesn't want to."

LeeAnn was one of Marlene's sisters. She had five.

"I thought it was only against the law if your religion wouldn't let you wear deodorant," I said.

"Uh-uh. Even if you just don't *want* to, they can't make you. LeeAnn says."

I didn't believe this, but I didn't argue. It was hard arguing with Marlene. She always thought she was the expert, with all those sisters.

"So what're you going to do?" I asked.

"Sue the school."

That was the good thing about Marlene. She always knew exactly what to do. Hanging out with her, I felt as if I did, too.

I stood on tiptoes and craned my neck, trying to see over the crowds of kids.

"Have you seen Travis? My friend Travis from next door?" I asked. Marlene had met him at some of my birthday parties.

"What's he doing here?" Marlene asked.

"He's going here this year. His father got transferred to Saudi Arabia," I explained. "I was thinking we could ask him to eat lunch with us."

Marlene sighed and rolled her eyes.

"Does he chew with his mouth open?" she asked. "I hate eating with boys."

"He won't know anyone."

"So? He'll make friends. Boy friends."

"It's hard being new," I said.

"How do you know? You've never been new." Marlene crossed her arms over her chest and looked away. "I'm not hanging around with some dumb old boy who chews with his mouth open just because he's new."

"You'd like him. He's not like other boys," I said.

"All boys stink," Marlene said. "And all girls know it."

Mom was always asking me who I thought was handsome because she was in a hurry for me to be the kind of girl she wanted: giggly and neat and sneaking looks at boys. To Marlene, though, part of being a girl was hating boys.

It was confusing, trying to keep both of them happy, trying to figure out which one was right.

Just then Marlene said, "Isn't that him?"

She was pointing to one of the basketball courts. I looked and saw a bunch of the fifth-grade boys. You could tell they were fifth graders because they were the tallest kids on the playground and they wore baseball caps with the visors pointing backward and shorts that came to below their knees.

Someone passed the ball to Travis. He stood stock-still for a second, his skinny sneakers pointing out, his bony white hands lightly on the ball. The breeze from one of the other players running made a lock of his hair flutter. He was wearing baggy blue-jean shorts and a huge T-shirt with a picture of Michael Jordan on it. New clothes: clothes I'd never seen. The shirt hung down almost to his knees.

"Pass it, Mooney!" some kid yelled.

Travis looked right, then left. Then he was running, hunched forward, the ball bee lining from his palm to the pavement and back again, like a yo-yo. I had no idea Travis was such a good dribbler.

He ran low to the ground, snaking in and out among the other boys, as if he was sneaking up on the basket. Finally, when he was close enough, he stopped, held the ball under his cheek and shut one eye, and then shot. The ball shushed through the hoop just as the bell rang.

Some kids cheered; some groaned. The boys playing basketball ran together, like a pack of animals, toward the halls. One of them gave Travis a high-five as he loped past him.

"Rats," Marlene said, hoisting her backpack over her shoulder. "Fourth grade. Rats."

We trudged toward the classrooms. All I could think of was how Travis had looked, eye-ing the basket, just before he'd let go of the ball. As though he was totally sure that the ball would go in. As though there wasn't even a question.

He did not look like a kid who would be lonely at lunch.

★ ★ ★

Marlene and I got Mrs. Dooley. Mrs. Dooley looked like everybody's grandmother except for her braces. Some of the kids called her Mrs.

Drooley behind her back. She said everything with a fake English accent.

Mrs. Dooley assigned us seats and talked about school rules and being kind on the playground and not spitting. She said that she always loved meeting new students and that we were going to have a great time learning and discovering together. Then she made us write down some spelling words.

I wondered how Travis was liking Miss Cox, and if he'd called her "Sister" by mistake, and what he thought of the girls in his class, and if the work was harder or easier than at his old school. And if he liked wearing regular clothes. And which kids he liked the best.

Remember everything, I thought. I couldn't wait for recess.

★ ★ ★

"So what'd you think?" I asked Marlene as we headed for our favorite bench. "Drooley's not so bad."

"Remahkable," Marlene said, imitating Mrs. Dooley. "Boy, does she get on my nerves."

"Maybe she really is English," I said.

"My mother says she's from New Jersey," Marlene said. "Come on. Let's sit in the shade."

Just then I saw Travis. He was between two fifth-grade boys, Jake Costello and Tony Freites. I didn't know Jake and Tony very well. They were laughing at something Travis was saying. I thought how weird it was that after two hours at Earl Cronkite Elementary School, Travis knew Jake and Tony better than I did after five whole years. It didn't seem fair. Actually, it seemed really crummy.

Travis saw me. His smile slid off his face, as if it had been pasted there. His eyes got big and darted back and forth, as if he was wishing there was some other way to go than toward me.

"How's it going?" I asked.

Travis looked at his shoes.

"OK," he mumbled.

"How's Miss Cox?"

"OK."

"Just OK?"

Tony leaned over and whispered something to Jake. They laughed like hyenas.

Travis hunched up his shoulders and dug his hands deeper into his pockets.

"Yeah. OK. You know," he said, shrugging, "just a teacher."

This wasn't like Travis. Travis liked teachers.

"Well, what's she *like*? Does she give out candy like Sister Beatrice? Does she say stuff like, 'A *roast* is done. *You* are finished'?"

"Yeah," Tony Freites said. He leaned toward Travis, holding his hands together in front of his chest. "What's she *like*, Travis?"

Travis turned bright red. He still wouldn't look up from his shoes.

"Shut up, Tony," I said. I knew when I was being made fun of.

Travis sighed.

"Jeez, Abigail," he said. He looked right at me. His face looked different from usual. "Just like any old teacher. I just said."

I stared in silence. Stunned.

"How many times I gotta say?" Travis said.

As though I was his mother reminding him about picking his clothes off the floor or something.

Jake punched Travis on the shoulder. I couldn't tell if it was a mean punch or an atta-boy punch.

"Hey," I said, suddenly remembering. "Where were you this morning?"

"What are you talking about?"

"I went to your house at eight-fifteen. You weren't there."

"Of course I wasn't there," Travis said. "I was here."

"But I thought—"

Jake grabbed Travis's arm and yanked him backward.

"We're not gonna get a court if you stand here yakking all day," he said.

Travis let himself be pulled away. After a second, Marlene said, "Travis Mooney. What a dumb name. Gooney Mooney. That's what we should call him. It's like I always say—boys are idiots. Boys are not even worth wasting breath talking to."

"Yeah," I said, mainly because I didn't feel like arguing.

We grabbed bench space under the maple tree and ate our snacks. Then we snagged a tetherball court and played three games. I won once. I didn't even look at the basketball courts to see if anyone had noticed.

★ ★ ★

I didn't see Travis anymore at school that day. Marlene and I ate lunch with some of the other fourth-grade girls. We checked pogo sticks and Hula-Hoops out of the ball room. I hadn't used a Hula-Hoop all summer. I was really rusty.

After school I went to Marlene's house. Usually I liked her more at school than at home. It was hard to play at her house because her sisters were all over the place. The two older ones wouldn't let us in the living room. The three little ones were always trying to butt into our games, and when we told Mrs. Jamison, she said we were the big girls and we had to play nice.

Finally we took our Parcheesi board and our bowl of popcorn and snuck into the garage.

"They're not allowed in here," Marlene said. "They'll never find us."

"I don't know how you stand it," I said.

"I don't, either."

"Don't you get sick of never being alone?" I asked. I couldn't imagine sharing a room.

"Yeah, but that's not the worst thing." Marlene jammed popcorn into her mouth. "The worst thing is knowing that they wish they'd had a boy. At least one boy."

"How do you know that?"

"Six girls? Who wants six girls?" Marlene licked salt off her lips. "You *know* they wish one of us had been a boy."

"My mom would've liked six girls," I said.

Six girls who liked to wear dresses and hairbands and pink nail polish. I didn't tell Marlene that part, though. She might have laughed at me, made fun of how I went around with holes in the knees of my jeans and sometimes forgot to comb my hair.

Marlene and I were better at playing than talking.

I checked my watch in the shadowy light of the garage. I wished it was time for Mom to pick me up. Sometimes it was a lot of work, being Marlene's friend. I had to be careful what I said. Make sure I didn't say too much.

I never had to be careful with Travis.

★ ★ ★

He was sitting on his front lawn when Mom pulled into the garage that afternoon. He was pulling up grass and stuffing it into his socks. He looked as if he was waiting for me.

"Hi, Phantom," he said as I got out of the car.

"Hi." I waited until Mom had walked out to the curb to get the mail. "So how was it?"

"Good. Fine. I like it. Miss Cox is great. She said we have to do handwriting, only not to worry if we're not very good at it because eventually we'll all be using computers anyway. She said in fifty years no one will even know what a pencil *is*."

"I like handwriting," I said. *Now Miss Cox is great,* I thought.

"I sit by the window. I like being able to see out. Miss Cox says I can daydream once in a while, as long as I finish all my work." He paused. "At St. Francis Prep I had to write 'I will not daydream' fifty times on the blackboard after school."

Usually I would have laughed.

"I like the kids. The boys, at least. Tony Freites can bend his fingers backward all the way to his wrist."

"He's the kind of kid who's always getting in trouble," I said. Everybody knew about Tony Freites. He had a reputation.

"I like him."

It was crummy, not agreeing.

"Jeez." Travis looked into his sock. I knew he wanted to quit talking. I could tell by the way he kept looking behind him, as if he was half hoping his mom would make him come inside to do his homework.

Something was different. I'd never been afraid

of Travis. But now, I was afraid to tell him how I almost cried when Tony and Jake had whispered and laughed.

I didn't tell him. Instead, I thought, *Be careful.*

Four

"Who knows who Sherlock Holmes was?" Mrs. Dooley asked on Friday.

Only Angela Peterson raised her hand. Angela Peterson raised her hand even when she didn't know the answer.

"Yes, Angela?" Mrs. Dooley said.

Angela jerked her hand back down.

"I forget," she said.

"Sherlock Holmes was a fictional character who solved mysteries," Mrs. Dooley said. "No matter how horrible the crime or how puzzling the clues, Sherlock Holmes was able to apply logic and reasoning to every situation. He solved the cases that no one else could solve."

Kenny Lipman raised his hand.

"Someone broke into the trunk of my uncle's car and stole a toolbox," he said. "The police never could catch him."

"Too bad Sherlock Holmes wasn't on the case,"

Mrs. Dooley said. "We'll be reading some Sherlock Holmes stories next week. Right now I want you to think about something mysterious that's been happening in your own life. Something you've wondered about but have been unable to figure out. Class? Who would like to share some ideas?"

Emily Thayer wondered where her cat slept at night. Joe Christophe wondered where the snails went after they ate the marigolds. Shanna Hoversten wondered what her mother put in the meatloaf.

"Try to pick a mystery that can't be solved just by asking someone for the answer," Mrs. Dooley said. "And think of something that doesn't involve spying on your parents."

After a few more kids had made suggestions, Mrs. Dooley said, "I'd like you all to give this some more thought over the weekend. Then next week each of you will write about your mystery and try to solve it. Think creatively. And remember, you must try to solve your mystery in a way that doesn't violate anyone's privacy."

"You mean we can't listen in on phone calls?" Marvin Sherwood asked.

"That is correct," Mrs. Dooley said. "And it goes without saying that you can't do anything dangerous or illegal."

Marlene passed me a note. *Is it violating my mother's privacy if I try to figure out what color her hair would be if she didn't dye it?*

Probably, I wrote back. I was worried. I couldn't think of anything mysterious in my life. Everything seemed boring and obvious.

"If it goes without saying—" Joe Christophe shouted out.

"I'm saying it anyway," Mrs. Dooley said sternly.

⭐ ⭐ ⭐

"What mystery are you going to do?" Marlene asked at lunch.

"I don't know," I said. "What if your life just isn't very mysterious?"

"Try living with five sisters," Marlene said. "Who broke the CD player? Who took my shin guards? Who read my diary?" She took a bite of her tuna sandwich. "There are a million mysteries at my house. Feel free to solve any one of them."

"Thanks, anyway, but I think I'll try to come up with one of my own," I said.

Just then Philip Cassavetes and Neil Chan sat down on the playground right in front of us. Philip started taking off one of his shoes and socks. Marlene and I looked at each other and rolled our eyes.

"This ought to be good," Marlene whispered.

"What are you doing?" I asked Philip.

"Showing Neil my toenail," Philip said.

"What's the big deal about your toenail?" Marlene asked.

"It's never been cut," Philip said.

"Oh, come on," I said. "That's impossible."

"No, it's not." Philip held his foot in our direction. "See? Never in nine whole years."

"Wow," Neil said.

"My dad hasn't cut one of his toenails in nine years, either. Just to keep me company," Philip said. "It's a Cassavetes tradition, he says."

"That is the most disgusting thing I've ever seen," Marlene said. "The way it curls under your foot."

"Isn't it hard to walk?" I asked.

Philip started to put his sock back on.

"You get used to it," he said proudly.

After the boys had gotten up and left, Marlene said, "I know a mystery that no one can solve. How come boys are such morons?"

"Not all boys," I said. I looked toward the basketball courts. I could just make Travis out. He was calling to Tony Freites and holding up his hands, as if he wanted the ball. Tony threw it to him, and Travis ran toward the hoop, trying for a slam-dunk. He missed by a mile. A couple of the fifth-grade boys laughed, but not in a mean way. More in a you're-one-of-us way.

"Remember when Nancy Bohanon moved here in second grade? And sat on the bench every day at recess not talking?" I asked.

Marlene nodded.

"How long did it take her to make friends?" I asked.

"I don't know. Maybe until Valentine's Day. A

★

★

long time," Marlene said. "I remember someone started a rumor that she was from Sweden and didn't speak English. I went up to her and asked her and she was so scared she didn't even answer, so I thought it was true. It took me a long time to figure out that she was just shy."

"Do you think it's different for boys?" I asked. "Do they just make friends faster?"

"Who knows? Maybe they just stick their disgusting old toenails in each other's faces if they can't think of anything to talk about. Maybe girls should do stuff like that."

"If Nancy Bohanon had stuck her foot in my face, it wouldn't have made me like her," I said. "It would have made me sick."

"That's the difference between girls and boys," Marlene said, swallowing the last of her sandwich.

"Talk about a mystery," I said.

★ ★ ★

I had barely seen Travis all week. At school I caught sight of him down the hallway or across the playground or at one of the other lunch tables. He was always surrounded by a group of fifth-grade boys. He was always laughing or pretend punching someone or sneaking up on other boys and burping as loudly as possible. It wasn't that he was mean to me or anything. He didn't even seem to notice me. Which, in a funny way, was almost worse.

It was different when Travis lived with his

dad. I barely saw him, but it wasn't because he wanted to play basketball with a bunch of creepy boys. He couldn't help not seeing me then. Now he wasn't seeing me on purpose.

It wasn't as if I didn't have other friends. Marlene, for one. And I liked a lot of the girls in my class—Emily and Shanna and Haley—even if I didn't know them very well.

Marlene was sort of a best friend. Sort of. I had lunch with her every day. She made me laugh like crazy. She knew what was fun. In first grade we snuck into the teachers' lounge at recess and listened while Miss Carp complained about her boyfriend having no money. In second grade we made a fort on the roof of her garage. We got stuck up there and had to wait for Mr. Jamison to get home from work and help us down.

We were always doing things that I would never have thought of on my own.

But how could you be best friends with someone who agreed with your mother about you wearing hairbows and lacy socks?

Travis laughed only at jokes, or when someone said something funny on TV. When he was supposed to.

★ ★ ★

When the doorbell rang on Saturday, I peeked out the front window and saw Travis standing at the door.

"You want to ride bikes down to the 7-Eleven and get Slurpees?" he asked when I opened the door.

"Can't. I have to baby-sit," I said.

"Baby-sit" meant I had to stay with Grandma while my mom went to the gym. I didn't say it in front of Grandma, though.

"Can I hang around?"

"Sure," I said, backing away from the door. The house was a mess. A pink basket full of clean clothes sat in the living room, waiting to be folded. The newspaper was spread out on the coffee table where Grandma had been reading it. A saucer full of toast crumbs and a half-drunk cup of coffee were on the floor by the table. Grandma wasn't very good about cleaning up after herself. I would have minded in front of Marlene. I'm the kind of person who likes things neat, especially in front of my friends. But I didn't mind so much with Travis. He understood about Grandma.

"You want to play Star Warrior?" I asked.

"Cool," Travis said.

We headed into the kitchen, where the computer was. I booted up the game. Travis hunted around for Oreos.

We were right in the middle of a battle for intergalactic domination when Grandma walked in.

"What's all the racket?" she asked crankily.

"Just a second, Grandma," I said. "We're right in the middle of a game."

"Don't 'Just a second' me," she said. She banged the floor with her cane. "Dammit."

Uh-oh, I thought. Grandma only said bad words when she was in a really grumpy mood. "Just keep playing," I whispered to Travis, "only don't make so much noise.

"You want some coffee, Grandma?" I asked. I tried to make my voice bright and springy.

"No coffee," she said. "They stole my bed!"

People with Alzheimer's are always thinking stuff like this. You get used to it after a while. The best thing to do is play along.

"Who stole your bed?"

"Those crooks! Those . . . ruffians!" Grandma's hands started to shake. She licked her lips a couple of times. She was really upset. "They think they can get away with it! Hah!"

"What should I do, Grandma? What do you want me to do?" Sometimes it helped, asking her for advice. It calmed her down.

Sometimes.

"What do you mean, 'What should I do?' Call the police! Darn fool kid," Grandma said.

I hesitated. I didn't want to call the police for real. They'd just laugh. And I didn't want to pretend to do it, either, all the while just talking to a dial tone. Grandma might grab the receiver away from me and try to talk. She'd know I'd lied, and there was no telling what she'd do then.

"Mrs. Van Fossen?" Travis was standing up, looking right at Grandma. His eyes were wide and serious. "I think they brought it back. Your bed."

Grandma looked at Travis with disbelief.

"Who's that?" she asked.

"Travis Mooney, ma'am." Travis gulped and blinked. "I saw them bringing your bed back just a few minutes ago."

Grandma squinted. "You sure?"

"Yes, ma'am."

Something in Grandma's shoulders sagged. I think it had been a long time since anyone had called her ma'am.

"We'll just see about that," Grandma said. "Come on, Frances."

Travis and I exchanged a look.

"Well, don't just stand there!" Grandma yelled. "Come hold my arm, Frances! And we'll just see about that darn fool bed!"

"Be back in a second," I said to Travis. Grandma felt spindly and shaky on my arm, like a wobbly bird.

I walked her down the hall to her room. Grandma's room was on the first floor, at the back of the house. It was full of old furniture and books and smelled like the back of a closet. It had a picture window that looked out over the back yard and let in a lot of sun. Mom was always saying that someday she wanted to take a hose to that room and turn it into a den. I knew what she meant by "someday" even though she never said.

"See, Grandma?" I said. I let her down carefully until she was sitting on the edge of the rickety twin bed with the worn white spread. "It's here. Just like Travis said. They must have brought it back."

Grandma gave a couple of measly bounces.

"I'm not so sure," she said suspiciously.

"About what?"

"About that fellow." Grandma squinted distrustfully. "I think he may have had something to do with this."

"Not Travis, Grandma." I tried to be patient. "Travis wouldn't take your bed. And besides, it's here. You're sitting on it."

Grandma shook her head.

"I'm not so sure," she said. But she didn't try to get up, and her sitting was a little like admitting she was wrong.

"You want to take a nap, Grandma? And I'll fix you something while you're resting. Some split-pea soup or something." Mom had just started letting me use the stove when she was out.

"You watch that Tom fellow," Grandma said. She meant Travis. She bounced again and the bedsprings creaked. "He's a shady character. Don't you get mixed up with him."

"I won't, Grandma," I said. I tried to sound soothing. "You take a rest. I'll make you some lunch."

"Darn fool ruffians," Grandma muttered, lying back against the spread. "I think they got my typewriter, too."

"Quick thinking, Speedy," I said as I reentered the kitchen.

Travis looked up from the computer.

"Thanks," he said. "I got us to Planet Zebular."

"Sometimes she's really bad like that," I said, leaning down and rummaging around in a cupboard for a pot. "Once she looked out the front window and saw Mr. Fisher across the street mowing his lawn. She called the police and told them that Martians had invaded the neighborhood."

Travis laughed. "I remember that."

"The weirdest thing was the time she couldn't find her purse. Mom and I looked everywhere for that purse. *Everywhere.* We looked under the couch cushions. I even looked behind the toilet. Then Mom thought maybe she'd left it in the car, so we ran outside to check. We were in the car for maybe two minutes. When we went back inside, Grandma was sitting at the kitchen table looking through her purse. 'Where was it?' Mom asked. Grandma looked at her like she had three heads. 'Where it always is,' she said. We never did figure out where. And Grandma had forgotten that it had been lost in the first place."

"I can't imagine not being able to remember like that," Travis said.

I loved it that he'd stopped laughing. I felt I could tell him anything.

"How come she calls you Frances?" Travis asked.

"I don't know. I've asked her. She never says. She just laughs, like I'm teasing her or playing a trick."

"Don't your parents know?"

I shook my head.

"It's a mystery," I said. "Hey!"

"What?"

"My project." I explained about Sherlock Holmes.

"Cool," Travis said. "In fourth grade *we* had to write book reports on Betsy Ross."

"I could figure out who Frances is," I said. Saying it out loud, I wasn't sure it was such a good idea. "I've been trying to figure this out for a long time, though. I don't know how I'm suddenly going to solve a mystery as tough as this one."

"Maybe writing down clues and really thinking about it will help," Travis said.

"Maybe." But I was still pretty doubtful.

"*I'll* help," Travis said.

Five

I got a piece of paper and a pen out of Mom's desk.

"What do we know so far?" Travis asked.

"OK." I stared out the kitchen window for a minute, thinking. "She's called me Frances for about a year. Since she got really bad."

"Does she know who anybody is?"

"Sometimes my dad, but mostly she thinks he's her brother Stewart. She thinks my mom is *her* mom. Sometimes she thinks the mailman is someone she knew in the war. Probably because of the uniform, my dad thinks."

"That makes sense," Travis said. "I mean, as much sense as anything."

"I know who Frances *isn't*," I said. "Grandma didn't have any daughters with Grandpa George. Or sisters, either. Her brother's wife is Betty. And they have two daughters, Elizabeth and Estelle."

"Maybe she had a baby who died," Travis said. "How many years was she married?"

"She married my grandpa when she was eighteen," I said. I added in my head. "Fifty-three years."

"A lot can happen in fifty-three years," Travis said. "Didn't a lot of babies die in the olden days?"

"She'd have told us. My dad would know."

"You never know everything about a person," Travis said. "It could be a distant cousin. It could be anyone."

The split peas were bubbling. I got up and turned the burner off. Then I ladled some soup into a bowl.

"Maybe you can ask her how the two of you met," Travis said. "Or what kinds of things you liked to do together. Maybe that'll give you a hint."

"I think she knew Frances in school," I said. "She was telling me I was good in biology." I blew on the soup and set the bowl on a tray. "What is biology anyway?"

"The study of life. How bodies work. You have to take biology if you want to be a doctor. Maybe Frances is a doctor."

"Well, that really narrows it down. There are only about a million doctors around."

"It's a start." Travis looked at the kitchen clock. "I have to go."

"Rats," I said. Baby-sitting Grandma was a slow way to spend a Saturday. "Are you going somewhere?"

"Yeah." Travis looked embarrassed.

"How come? Did your mom and Donald decide you need some QT?"

QT was "quality time." Mr. and Mrs. Blankenship spent a lot of time wondering if Travis was getting enough of it.

"Nah." Travis shook his head. "I've just got to go somewhere."

"Where?"

"Just somewhere." He fidgeted around in his chair. "Tony Freites's house."

"Oh." I pulled a spoon out of the drawer. In San Francisco Travis had other friends. Marshall and Wizard and other boys, too. It had never bothered me before.

"We're just going to play basketball. And maybe do some homework. Tony has trouble with math."

"Tony Freites is disgusting."

"He's really OK," Travis said.

"I don't like him," I said stubbornly. For some reason, I reminded myself of Marlene.

"He's funny. He's great at basketball. He knows all this cool stuff about spontaneous combustion. You know, when people catch fire and burn up and no one can figure out why." Travis smiled. "I think he's finally starting to like me."

"Since when do you care who's great at basketball?"

"I love basketball," Travis said.

"You do?"

Travis nodded.

"It's my favorite thing to do at school," he said. "Marshall and Wizard and I always played basketball at recess."

"I hate basketball," I said, feeling rotten.

Weren't best friends supposed to like the same things?

Travis shrugged. "I don't care. As long as I get to play. As long as my friends at school like to play." He started backing out into the hall. "We can still be friends at home," he said.

I didn't know how to be "friends at home." You were either friends everywhere, all the time, or not friends.

"So I'll see you around, Phantom," he said.

I felt like telling him not to call me that. The day we'd come up with those nicknames, I thought I knew everything there was to know about Travis Mooney. Now I felt as though I didn't know a thing.

★ ★ ★

"I put an ice cube in it, so it'd cool," I said, setting the tray down on the table by the bed.

Grandma looked up from a piece of paper she'd been reading. "Eh? What's that?" she asked. She folded the paper into a little square and slipped it into the pocket of her dress.

An old letter, I thought. I was curious. Suddenly everything about Grandma seemed interesting.

"Split-pea soup," I said. I held out my hand

and Grandma grabbed at it, steadying herself and arranging her feet so they touched the floor. She leaned forward and sniffed the steam rising off the soup.

"Where's my napkin?" she said. Still grumpy. I pulled a square of paper towel off a roll that sat on her bureau and handed it to her, and she tucked it under her chin. Then she fumbled with the spoon, leaned even closer to the soup, and began to eat.

I waited until she'd managed to get a few spoonfuls into her mouth.

"Grandma?" I asked. "How'd we meet?"

My stomach felt shivery.

Grandma looked up.

"How's that?" she said.

"I said, 'How'd we meet?' Do you remember?"

Grandma nodded, but then she said, "It was a long time ago."

"How long?"

"Long enough." She dipped her head again and pursed her lips at her spoon.

"Well, but when? Were you a kid?" Pause. "Were we kids?"

Grandma slurped soup and licked her lips. I thought maybe she hadn't heard me, but then she said, "That Mrs. MacGuinness was a card, all right."

I sighed. This was hopeless. "Who's Mrs. MacGuinness?"

Grandma set her spoon in the bowl.

"I remember standing in the hallway and saying loud as you please, 'She's OK except for being so hairy.'" Grandma laughed: a squeaky, wheezing sound. "And she came up on us just like that. 'Miss Winkler,' she said, 'I'll see you in my office!'"

"Was I there, Grandma?" An office. Maybe Mrs. MacGuinness was a principal.

Grandma looked at me. She had a dribble of split-pea soup on her chin, but she really looked at me. Like she was really seeing me. It happened every once in a while. Not so often now. It made me remember how things used to be: how we'd watched Miss America on TV and laughed at how silly the ladies looked in bathing suits and high heels; how we'd made chocolate pudding from scratch on rainy Sundays; how we'd sat outside on summer nights and counted stars. It made me miss her.

"Of course you were," Grandma said. "You were always there."

I heard the kitchen door open and close. "I'm home," Mom called.

Grandma sat up and reached for her square of paper towel.

"I can't eat this," she said, even though the bowl was almost empty. She looked as though she was getting ready to take a nap.

I took the tray with the dirty bowl and spoon back to the kitchen. Mom was listening to the answering-machine messages. She was wearing bright blue tights and a leotard with pink and yellow daisies all over it that looked more like curtains than something to wear. Her bangs were pulled off her face with a white terry-cloth headband.

"Where's Grandma?" she asked, pausing the machine.

"Sleeping. I made her some soup," I said.

"Good." She turned back to her messages. "Maybe I can get some vacuuming done."

Grandma didn't like the vacuum. Sometimes she thought it was an air-raid siren and made me crawl under the kitchen table.

Mom finished with the messages. Then she turned to me with a happy, I-have-exciting-news-for-you expression on her face.

"I signed you up for something today," she said.

Uh-oh.

"What do you mean 'signed me up'?" I hate being signed up for things I don't know about.

"They're offering a junior aerobics class at the gym. For girls just your age. It meets on Saturday mornings for an hour."

"Aerobics? Is that ladies jumping up and down and sweating?"

Mom nodded.

"I thought we could run out to the mall this afternoon and buy you some cute exercise clothes. It's more fun to do aerobics in pretty leotards."

"I'm not sure about aerobics," I said. "Don't I get enough exercise running at school and riding my bike?"

"Honey." Mom sounded exasperated. "It's not just exercise. It's fun dancing to all that music. And wearing those clothes. Aren't you tired of baggy jeans and shorts?"

"No."

Mom checked her watch. "When did Grandma lie down?"

"About five minutes ago."

"Good." Mom smiled. "We've got just enough time to dash over to the stores."

At the mall we bought a purple leotard and purple tights. Mom wanted me to try on an outfit that looked like a two-piece bathing suit, but I said no.

"It'll show off your nice, flat stomach," she said.

"I'd be embarrassed with all my skin hanging out," I said.

Mom shook her head as she held the clothes out in front of her.

"I wish I could wear something like this," she said.

"Why don't you?"

"Oh, no." Mom hung the outfit back on the rack. "I'm too old for this kind of thing."

She smiled in kind of a sad way and pulled another leotard off the rack.

"Are you sure you wouldn't like to try something in pink?" she asked.

"I hate pink," I said. "I have never worn any-thing pink in my whole life. Not since I was a baby."

"You were such a cute baby." Mom sighed. "All your lovely curly hair."

"I like my hair more now," I said. "I hated it long. It was always in the way."

"It's too bad you won't wear skirts," Mom said, turning to another rack. "These are absolutely darling."

⭐ ⭐ ⭐

In the car on the way home I asked, "Where did Grandma go to school?"

"She didn't go to college," Mom said. "Your dad was the first person in his family to do that."

"No, I mean high school. Or even before," I said.

"Well," Mom said, thinking. "It must have been in Michigan. She and Grandpa didn't move to Chicago until after World War II, I think. That's where your dad was born."

"Where in Michigan?"

"Someplace outside of Detroit. Why all this interest in Grandma?"

"I'm trying to figure out who Frances is. For a school project."

"That's a pretty funny project."

"We have to solve a mystery without violat-ing anybody's privacy. And Frances is the biggest mystery I can think of," I said. "I'm pretty sure she's someone Grandma knew in school."

"How'd you come up with that?"

"She told me about some lady named Mrs. MacGuinness who called her into her office. And she said I—I mean, Frances—was there when it happened." I leaned forward and cranked up the air conditioner. "I was thinking that maybe Mrs. MacGuinness was a principal at one of Grandma's schools."

"That sounds possible."

"Isn't there some way to check? Someone to ask?"

"Maybe Dad would know. Ask him," Mom said.

I sighed as we turned off the freeway. What would Sherlock Holmes do? Asking people wasn't getting me anywhere.

"I wish Grandma didn't have Alzheimer's," I said. *Dumb old Grandma,* I thought. Even though I knew it wasn't her fault.

"It's a terrible disease," Mom said.

"*I'm* not getting it," I said.

"Did you know that your grandma worked for forty years, when lots of women stayed home and raised their children? And she used to adopt stray animals. Did you know that?" Mom flicked her blinker on. "And she was quite an athlete. She used to run three miles a day before anybody even knew what aerobics was."

"It's hard to believe," I said. "Her legs look like pencils."

"Grandma never planned on getting Alzheimer's," Mom said quietly. "Nobody does."

"I'm just not getting it, that's all," I said.

"Sometimes things happen," Mom said as we turned into the driveway. "Unimaginable things."

"Not to me."

"Things we can't do anything about," Mom said.

She turned the car off. I felt all mixed up. How could a crummy thing like Alzheimer's happen to Grandma, who'd always been so smart and strong? How come Mom sounded so nice when she talked about Grandma but got on my nerves when she tried to buy me clothes?

I slammed the car door shut, thinking, *If I feel mixed up, just think how it must be for Grandma.*

Six

On Monday the sky was blue like a flame. It was going to be hot, so hot that shade wouldn't matter. I couldn't find clean socks or a T-shirt I liked; I had to settle for a shirt with a giant Easter egg on it. Dad was already gone, and Mom was grumpy about being out of cereal and about my wearing an out-of-season shirt.

I was sweaty and red by the time I got to school. Mrs. Dooley was cross because I had turned in crumpled homework on Friday. "Let's not get off to a bad start, Abigail," she said. It wasn't as bad as being yelled at, but it still felt crummy.

"Don't even talk to me," I told Marlene at lunch. "I'll sit with you, but I'm not talking."

"You're not the only one having a bad day," Marlene said. "The boys at my science table were having the stupidest discussion I've ever heard."

"What about?"

"Simon was saying that when they cut your

head off you live for two more seconds, and Philip said wouldn't it be cool if after they did it they held you up in front of a mirror so you could see what you looked like while you were just a head."

"That is totally disgusting," I said.

"Then Joe wondered what would happen if you were chewing something and swallowed it right before they cut your head off. If chewed-up food would just fall out of the bottom of your neck."

"Why are you telling me this?"

"Boys are sickening. They shouldn't even be allowed to live in the same state we do," Marlene said.

"Not all boys," I said.

"How come you're always defending them?" Marlene said. "It's because of that stupid Travis Mooney. Gooney Mooney. The one you like."

"Not *like* like," I said.

"What's so great about him, anyway? He's another dumb old boy," Marlene said.

"You don't even know him," I said. "He's funny and smart. He's great to talk to."

"I hate his elbows. The way they're all bloody and scabby."

"You can't not like someone because of his elbows!"

"I don't like him because he's a *boy!*" Marlene yelled. Then, quietly, she said, "You always want to just talk."

"Forget it. *Forget* it." I said. I stood up. "It's too hot to sit here. I'm going to the library."

"Who cares?" Marlene said.

How did we end up fighting? I thought.

"You can come, if you want," I said.

"Who wants to sit in the library at lunch?" Marlene said. "You never want to do anything fun."

"Fine!"

I turned and stomped off toward the library. To get there, I had to walk around the basketball court. I could see Travis standing at the three-point line: crouching a little, aiming, shooting. He missed and thumped his thigh with his fist. He didn't look too upset, though.

Then he saw me. Even though he was already red from playing basketball, he got redder. He looked down at his shoes.

"Hi, Speedy," I said.

We can still be friends at home, I thought. Did that mean I couldn't say hi to him at school?

He grunted. It might have been "Hi," but it was hard to tell. He looked at the ground and kicked at rocks that weren't there.

"Listen, Travis, I thought—"

"Hey, Mooney!" Tony Freites yelled. "Is that your girlfriend?"

"Shut up," Travis said, but not as though he was defending me.

"Yes, it is. Abigail Van Fossen. I know her. She is so your girlfriend," Tony said.

"I'm nobody's girlfriend," I said. I was surprised he even knew my name. "You don't know anything about me!"

"I know lots of stuff about you," Tony said. "Your mother and my mother take the same exercise class. I know *everything* about you!"

"You don't know anything," I said, but I wasn't as sure as I sounded. My mother could be a big talker.

"I know you have a crazy grandmother," Tony said.

"She's not crazy!" I yelled.

"Yes, she is." Tony dribbled the ball three times. The boys who'd been playing basketball were crowding around behind him. "She thinks it's 1943. She eats dog food and yells at the mailman."

At first I thought only a few of the boys were laughing.

"She's sick!" I said. "She has a disease!"

"She thinks that the food is poisoned in restaurants and President Nixon stole her shoes." Tony was looking at his friends on the court. "She's wacko!"

They were all laughing. Every one of them.

Even Travis. As if he'd just heard the funniest joke of all time.

I couldn't believe it.

I glared at Tony Freites.

"She is not!" I yelled. "You jerk!"

"Ooooh!" Tony danced around the bouncing ball. "Your girlfriend's mad at me, Mooney! Hey! Maybe she's as wacko as her grandma!"

I was so mad that I could hardly see.

"What are you gonna do? Tell your wacko

grandma to bite me?" Tony was laughing so hard, he had to grab his stomach.

I looked at Travis.

"Thanks," I said. "Thanks a whole lot."

I felt as though it was the last time I would ever see him, as though he was getting on a plane and never coming back.

I made myself talk quietly so only Travis could hear. "I wish you *had* moved to Saudi Arabia," I said.

Travis stopped laughing. There was only a little bit of a smile left on his face. He shook his head, almost as if the smile was a bug he was trying to shake off.

"Oh, come on," he said. "It *is* pretty funny, how she's scared of the dishwasher."

I turned and walked away. I heard some of the fifth-grade boys laughing and the sound of the dribbling ball. I felt totally alone.

The bell rang. All the kids talking and yelling around me sounded like water rushing in my ears: sound that didn't mean anything, sound without words. I saw some third-grade girls giggling, hunched close together. I felt bad for them. You'll be sorry, I wanted to say.

In class I tried to pay attention to Mrs. Dooley, but she was talking about how to write a topic sentence, and I felt my eyelids getting heavy. To keep myself awake I thought about my mystery. How could I find out more about Frances? I could call my aunt Betty in Chicago. She might know something. She was really my dad's aunt, not mine. Her arms were all veiny from lifting weights. I liked Aunt Betty.

The bell rang. I gathered up my books and stuffed them in my backpack. I saw Marlene grab her things and run out of the classroom. She hadn't passed me one note all day.

★
62
★

Seven

"How's my girl?" Aunt Betty said. Yelled was more like it. Aunt Betty was going deaf. She always yelled; she said she liked hearing what came out of her mouth because sometimes it wasn't the same as what she'd meant to say.

"OK," I said. "How's Dave?"

Dave was Aunt Betty's cat. He weighed seventeen pounds and had three legs. The other leg had gotten caught in the clothes dryer. Aunt Betty still couldn't figure out how Dave got in there.

"Dave's great!" Aunt Betty roared. "You sound lousy."

"I'm fine. I wanted to ask you something," I said. "Something about Grandma."

"What about her? She isn't calling those numbers on TV again, is she?"

Sometimes Grandma called psychics and tried to get them to tell her about the future. Once she called the Home Shopping Network and ordered five hundred dollars' worth of dolls.

"Not for a while," I said. "This is about when Grandma was in school."

"You mean high school?"

"Yeah. Or even grammar school. I'm not sure."

"Well, honey, I didn't know her then. Your uncle Stewart and I didn't get married until after the war," Aunt Betty said.

"I know. But I thought maybe you'd know something. About who her friends were."

"Well, now, let me see." Aunt Betty sounded like she was sitting down and getting ready for a nice long chat. "Lucille and Stewart were only a year apart in high school. They palled around with some of the same kids, I think."

"This is about a girl. A girl named Frances," I said.

"Frances . . . Frances." Aunt Betty was thinking. "Don't recall the name. What about her?"

"I'm just trying to figure out who she was," I said. "Grandma calls me that sometimes."

"Frances?"

"She won't say why. And Mom and Dad don't know."

"Ah! A mystery!" Aunt Betty laughed. "I love a good mystery."

"A good mystery's one you can solve."

"Frances . . . Hmm. I'm just not coming up with anything, Abigail. Have you looked in Lucille's high school yearbook?"

"I didn't even know she had one."

"Why, sure she does. Ask if you can see it."

"The only thing, Aunt Betty—she won't know where it is. You should see her room."

"Messy, huh?" Aunt Betty harrumphed. "That's funny. She was always an orderly woman, Lucille was. Meticulous."

"What's that?"

"Tidy. Well, how 'bout I send you your uncle Stewart's yearbook? I've got it here somewhere. And they were only a year apart. How would that be?"

From somewhere upstairs Mom yelled, "Abigail! Do you know what this is costing us?"

"That would be great, Aunt Betty."

"Will you send it back to me after you're finished with it? I like to hang on to Stewart's things. He'd have liked that."

"I promise," I said.

"He'd have known this Frances, that's for sure. My Stewart never forgot a name," Aunt Betty said. "How're your folks?"

"OK. Dad's working too much. Mom's up to forty-five minutes on the StairMaster."

"Good for her. She bench-pressing one fifty yet?"

I laughed.

"You want to talk to her?" I asked.

"Not this time. You've been on long enough. It's driving her batty, I'm sure." Aunt Betty laughed, then quieted down. "You sure you're all right? You sound funny."

"It's all this Frances stuff," I said. "It makes me feel—" I paused, thinking how to say it. "Not myself."

"You're yourself, all right. Take my word for it. Or don't take my word, take your own," Aunt Betty said. "That's the best thing. You know who you are."

"I guess."

"That's the important thing," Aunt Betty yelled. As if she meant it. As if it was the only thing that really mattered.

★ ★ ★

The week dragged on. Every day I waited for the mail, but the yearbook didn't come. I felt like Grandma waiting for her packages.

In class Mrs. Dooley talked more about Sherlock Holmes. "'He appears to have a passion for definite and exact knowledge,'" she read from *A Study in Scarlet*. She looked up from the book and out at the class over her glasses. "We should all be more like Sherlock Holmes," she said.

Sherlock Holmes and his friend Dr. Watson met and decided to live together at the beginning of *A Study in Scarlet*. They told each other all their bad qualities so that neither of them would be surprised or mad later on. "It's just as well for two fellows to know the worst of one another before they begin to live together," Sherlock Holmes said. He got depressed and liked to play with poisons. He asked Dr. Watson what was wrong with him.

Mrs. Dooley stopped reading and looked up at us again. "Have you ever told your friends your worst qualities?" she asked.

What friends? I thought.

"We tend to think about our friends' worst qualities rather than our own," Mrs. Dooley said. "What would you say *your* worst qualities are?"

I had to think about that. Mom would say my worst qualities were not hurrying enough and not caring about how I looked. Marlene hated the way I wouldn't race with her or arm-wrestle or try to beat her at chess or Scrabble. I said I hated being competitive, but Marlene thought I was just afraid of losing.

Also, not wanting to do anything fun. And not combing my hair. A lot of things, actually.

That was what they didn't like about me. I wasn't sure what I didn't like about myself.

"I am impatient with Mr. Dooley when he leaves wet towels on the bathroom floor. And I am lazy about exercise," Mrs. Dooley said.

I didn't know what Travis would say my worst qualities were. Being a girl. Being in fourth grade. Having a crazy family was probably in there, too. Everything that made me *me*.

★ ★ ★

I got used to being alone at school. Actually I wasn't

totally alone. I ate lunch with Amber Seavey and Yvonne Michaelson. Amber asked me what mystery I was doing. I told her that I was still trying to decide. I didn't want to take a chance on her making fun of Grandma. Amber was trying to figure out why her cat had gotten so fat. Yvonne wanted to know what her older brother kept stashed in garbage bags on the top shelf of his closet. Her mother had said to let her know if Yvonne ever figured it out.

After we finished lunch, we played hop-scotch. I kept wondering whether they would laugh if they knew my grandmother thought the vacuum cleaner was an air-raid siren and made me crawl under the kitchen table, if they thought it was abnormal to be friends with all boys or just the creepy ones.

You could know a million people in your life, and only a few would end up really being friends. It was a lot of work, weeding all the others out.

Was Frances someone Grandma had weeded out? I hadn't thought of that. I kept thinking she must have been important for Grandma to remember her. She had to have been somebody special. I hoped so, anyway. I didn't like the idea of Grandma mixing me up with just any old person.

Did I look like her? Is that why Grandma called me by her name? Why did she remember Frances and not somebody else? What was it about *Frances*?

What happened to people who got Alzheimer's

and couldn't remember their old friends? Or maybe didn't have any to begin with? Did they just make up names to call their granddaughters? That made me think of something else. What if there was no Frances? Or what if Grandma was just remembering someone whose name was really something else, Francine or Francesca, maybe?

I went into class every afternoon without any better idea of who Frances might be. But I knew two things. One was that I really wanted to know who she was. I couldn't believe that Grandma had called me Frances for a year and that I'd never much cared who she thought I was. Now I really wanted to know.

The other thing I knew was that figuring out Frances would have been a lot easier with someone to talk to. Even Sherlock Holmes had had Dr. Watson.

★ ★ ★

"You want me to watch Grandma?" I asked as Mom walked down the hallway past my room. It was Saturday. Mom was wearing her pink leotard, bright yellow tights, and wrinkly white socks.

"Not today," Mom said. "Today's junior aerobics, remember?"

Rats, I thought. I'd forgotten all about junior aerobics. The idea of jumping around with a bunch of strange kids to loud music sounded horrible. But I knew Mom would not want to hear this.

"I'll be hot," I said. "I won't know anyone."

"You'll make new friends."

"What about Grandma?"

"Mrs. Baxter from the Hospitality Center is going to sit with her while we're gone."

"But I—"

"I don't have time for this, Abigail. And you need to get dressed. We're going to be late."

I sighed and dragged myself off the bed. The only thing worse than having to go to a class I wasn't interested in was getting there late.

At the gym Mom pointed me in the direction of the fitness room.

"Would you like me to walk you in?" she asked.

"No." That would be the worst thing of all, I decided. Being late *and* being introduced to the teacher by your mother.

"Well, all right, then." Mom fussed with my leotard, which had gotten twisted. "Have fun, sweetie. Do your best. *Breathe.*"

"I hate breathing."

"Do it anyway." Mom put her hands on her hips and sighed. "Listen, Abigail. Try to enjoy this."

Was not enjoying stuff one of my bad qualities?

The fitness room was full of girls. There were probably twenty of them, but because I didn't recognize anyone it seemed as though there were more. They were stretching: touching the floor without bending their knees, pointing and unpointing their toes, sliding their legs apart into splits. A lot of the girls looked like teenagers, with makeup and earrings and nail polish and loud laughs.

"What are you doing here?"

Marlene was wearing a black leotard and blue sweatpants, and her hair was pulled into a ponytail with a terry-cloth wristband.

I couldn't believe it.

"My mom signed me up," I said.

"You hate this stuff."

"My mom says I might like it. What are *you* doing here? You don't like exercise unless it's something you can beat somebody at."

"*My* mom doesn't understand about that part," Marlene said. "She just wants to get rid of me for an hour."

"Hey, guys?" A lady at the front of the room was talking into a microphone strapped around her head. "My name's Tammy, OK? Let's get started?"

Tammy was too old to be a teenager, but probably not old enough to have any kids of her own. She made a lot of sentences sound like questions, so she sounded as if she wasn't very sure of anything she said, and also as if she was a little afraid of us.

She flipped a switch on a boom box sitting in the corner of the room, and loud, static-y dance music blared over us. Marlene and I looked at each other and rolled our eyes.

"We'll start out with some stretching?" Tammy reached above her head and took a deep breath. "Everybody breathe, OK?"

Marlene and I both stretched and breathed. Tammy had to keep reminding everyone about the breathing.

After we were all stretched out, Tammy made us run in place and do dumb things with our arms. All the while we were doing it she called out to us to do it more. She also hooted and whooped and sang along with the music and asked us if we were having any fun yet. I was dying to say no.

It started to get really hot in that room. Everybody was jumping and waving their arms and trying to move the way Tammy told us to. Even Tammy was red and shiny looking. She kept waving at her face and saying "Hot enough for ya?" and laughing when nobody answered. She smiled every second. Every single second. With sweat dripping off her forehead and everything. I couldn't get over it. Sweating always puts me in a really rotten mood.

"Everybody get a drink, OK?" she finally said, and we all went to our water bottles. I could have drunk for an hour. Mostly it was just nice to stand still.

"How's your mystery?" Marlene asked after she'd taken a sip of water.

I explained to Marlene about Frances. Marlene looked interested. "My aunt Betty's sending me my grandma's old yearbook. Maybe I'll find Frances in there." I breathed deeply, trying to get my heart to slow. "What mystery are you doing?"

"I'm trying to figure out where my Disneyland T-shirt is. I think one of my sisters spilled something on it and threw it away, but I've interviewed them and they all say no. Sandra acted suspicious, though."

"That's cool about the interviewing."

Marlene nodded.

"I haven't seen you with Gooncy Mooney lately," she said.

"So?" I was surprised Marlene had even noticed.

"Just that Gooney's always playing basketball and sitting on the fifth-grade boys' bench at lunch."

"So?"

"I haven't seen you with him, that's all."

"We hang out after school," I said. I didn't feel like telling Marlene what a creep Travis had turned out to be. I didn't like her being so nosy.

"Come on, guys?" Tammy called from the front of the room. "Don't drink too much, or you'll get a cramp, OK?"

"Oh, brother," Marlene said. "I'd like to cramp *her.*"

★ ★ ★

"I want you to give it one more try," Mom said as we turned onto Red Valley Drive.

"Mom—" But I stopped. I didn't know how to say what I felt.

I wanted to like junior aerobics. I knew she wanted me to.

"Look," Mom said. "Whether you like it or not, you have to finish this class. It's for your own good."

"But why?"

"Because exercise is good for you." She stopped, then smiled, as if she was trying to make a joke. "I don't know what the big deal is. Most girls love aerobics."

I slumped down in my seat.

"It's not fair," I mumbled.

"Life's not fair," Mom said as we bumped to a stop in our driveway.

"Well, it should be."

"Well, it isn't."

I almost said something really nasty, but then I thought of Marlene saying, "I'd like to cramp *her*." Thinking it was almost as good as saying it.

I was getting out of the car when I heard Mom say, "Hi, Travis."

"Hi, Mrs. Van Fossen," Travis said.

He looked the same—straight black hair, freckly white skin, long feet, scabbed-up knees and elbows—only different. I stared at him, trying to figure out what it was. Everything on the outside was the same.

"Hey, Abigail," he said.

As if nothing was wrong. That's what killed me.

"What do *you* want?" I said.

Mom looked back at us over her shoulder as she headed for the front door.

"Come in and change before you go out to play," she said.

I waited until she'd closed the door behind her.

"I'm not playing with you," I said. "Now or ever."

"I don't see what you're so upset about—"

"I'm not upset," I said. I was, but I didn't want Travis Mooney knowing about it.

"He was just starting to like me," Travis said.

Now I knew why Travis looked different. It was because I didn't like him anymore.

"Get lost, Mooney. Gooney Mooney."

Travis looked down at his shoes and shoved his fists in his pockets.

"I don't even want you on my driveway. Or breathing anywhere close to me," I said.

Travis looked up.

"You can't tell me to stop breathing," he said. His eyes were shiny. "You don't own the air!"

"If it's over my driveway I do." It was funny. It sounded like a stupid fight, like the ones I used to have with Marlene in first grade over whose turn it was to use the red chalk. But it wasn't stupid. I felt mad and powerful. I knew I was right.

"I hate your guts," I said.

"Good!" Travis yelled, but he was crying, too. I could see. "That's fine with me!"

"Dumb old crybaby boy," I said. "Just wait'll I tell Marlene how you cry like a sissy."

"See if I care!"

"Just wait'll I tell her how your creepy father hates you so much that he had to move to Saudi Arabia to get away from you."

My heart was thudding hard in my chest. I was scaring myself with how mean I was being.

"I know bad things about you, Travis Mooney. Don't forget about *that*," I said. "Like how your mom called you Mr. Pooper until you were six! Remember?"

"That's not fair!" Travis shouted.

Life's not fair.

"Don't think I wouldn't tell," I said. "Don't even *think* that."

"You don't understand—"

"Because I will." I wasn't even yelling anymore. I didn't need to yell. "I'll tell everyone everything," I said, "and there's nothing you can do."

Travis turned and walked back to his house. His shoulders sagged as though he was carrying something, even though his hands—hard, clenched balls at his sides—were empty.

Eight

"What was that all about?" Mom asked as I came into the kitchen.

"Nothing," I said. "Is the mail here?"

"It just came," Mom said. "There's a package for you."

The yearbook was called *The Blue and Silver* even though the school Grandma went to was William Howard Taft High. You could tell it was from a long time ago because all the pictures were in black and white, and the kids were wearing old-fashioned clothes and looked like grownups. There were a lot of pictures of kids sitting in a huge high-ceilinged auditorium and in front of a three-story brick building that looked more like a city hall than a school. I got the same feeling I always got when I looked at pictures taken a long time ago: that it was always cloudy back then. I wondered what the kids looked like now—white-haired, bent over, deaf, wrinkled—and how many of them were dead.

I found Uncle Stewart's picture first. He was in the section of the book set aside for eleventh graders. His picture was so small that it was hard to see what he had really looked like. I'd only met Uncle Stewart a couple of times before he died. He was tall and quiet and seemed as if he wasn't sure how to be around a kid. Mostly he let Aunt Betty do all the talking.

Grandma's picture was in the seniors' section. I found her—Lucille Winkler—on page thirty-six. I stared hard at her picture, trying to see Grandma in the girl with curly dark hair and twinkly eyes who smiled out at the camera. It was hard. Grandma's hair was gray now, and her eyes were hardly ever twinkly. In the picture she wore a white blouse with a V-neck and no makeup or jewelry.

I tried to decide if Grandma had been pretty, if she was the kind of girl that other girls thought was pretty. I couldn't be sure. Her hair was so old-fashioned looking. She had full cheeks and a pudgy neck: you couldn't see her body, but she looked as though she might be a little chubby. Girls today would have thought she looked dorky with no makeup. But there was something about her. She looked like the kind of girl who laughed a lot, who liked a good joke.

Who was always doing fun stuff.

Next to each senior's picture was a list of the clubs they'd belonged to, funny things they'd said, things people thought of when their names were mentioned. Next to Grandma's picture it said:

Lucille Mae Winkler, Our Kinda Gal, Student Leadership, Future Secretaries of America, Drama Club (Remember *Our Town*?). Most Likely to Keep a Fella Guessing. Favorite Book: *Sister Carrie*. Favorite Expression: "Gee whillikers!" What We'll Remember: Those pearly whites. What She'll Remember: "Bathing Beauties"; fudge sundaes on Saturdays; trips into town; chaperones.

Rats, I thought. I'd been hoping that Frances would be listed under "What She'll Remember." I wondered if Grandma remembered anything about high school now.

I turned to the section marked *Administration.* Sure enough, there was a picture of Mary MacGuinness under the heading *Our Beloved Principal.* She didn't look so hairy, not as far as I could see. *But she* was *the principal,* I thought. That meant Grandma and Frances had been standing in the hallway together in high school.

Her picture had to be in the yearbook!

It took me almost an hour. I checked the senior girls first. I found twenty-two Katharines and twelve Margarets and seven Elaines and six Lillians. Plus some names I'd never heard before, like Bertha and Ethel and Gladys and Mavis. No Tiffanys. No Chelseas.

★ ★ ★

I finished with the freshmen just as Mom came in from the kitchen.

"Not one Frances," I said.

"Maybe she was absent on picture day," Mom said.

"They list the absent ones at the back," I said. "I already checked. No Frances there."

"So it wasn't someone she knew in school," Mom said. "Maybe it was a friend in her neighborhood. Or someone who went to a different school." She looked over my shoulder. "Girls didn't wear pants back then. I always forget."

"I'll bet not one of them had a tattoo," I said. "Maybe Frances was someone Grandma knew in elementary school who moved away." But then why did Grandma remember standing in the hall outside Mrs. MacGuinness's office with Frances? Unless she was just plain crazy. Unless even the few things she did remember were all mixed up.

I sighed. The whole thing seemed hopeless.

"Where's your *A Study in Scarlet?*" Mom asked. "See if there's anything in there to help you."

I went to the kitchen door where my backpack sat on the shelves. I pulled out my copy of *A Study in Scarlet*. Its front cover was crinkled and bent and someone had drawn stars and question marks on the binding. I hoped Mrs Dooley wouldn't think it was me.

I plunked back down on the couch and

thumbed through the first few pages. "What about this?" I said, and read:

> "By a man's finger-nails, by his coat-sleeve, by his boots, by his trouser-knees, by the callosities of his forefinger and thumb, by his expression, by his shirt-cuffs—by each of these things a man's calling is plainly revealed."

I closed the book in my lap.

"What's 'callosities'? I don't get this," I said.

"What it means is, you have to look at every little thing," Mom said.

"Grandma doesn't wear boots," I said.

"That doesn't matter." Mom pointed at the paragraph I'd read. "Sherlock Holmes means you have to pay attention. Every little thing is a clue."

"How can it be a clue that Grandma went to high school with eighty-nine girls and not one of them was named Frances?" I asked.

"Beats me," Mom said. "You're the detective."

I sighed. But I knew she was right. I knew that if I just looked hard enough, I'd be able to figure out Frances.

And if I could figure out Frances—if I could undertand what it was about me that reminded Grandma of her—then maybe I could figure out myself a little bit, too.

On Monday Mrs. Dooley passed out permission slips and medical forms for the upper-class overnight.

"Have your parents sign these and return them to me as soon as possible," she said. "And these medical-release forms are important. We need to know if there is food you can't eat or activities you can't participate in while you're at camp."

"I'm allergic to nuts," Shanna Hoversten called out.

"Once when we went camping I got stung on my neck by a bee," Joe Christophe said. "It looked like I'd swallowed a golf ball."

"All important information we need *on your forms*," Mrs. Dooley said. "Please don't call out."

Amber raised her hand.

"Avocados give me hives," she said. "Is that something you need to know?"

"Not in the strictest sense, although it's very interesting," Mrs. Dooley said. "Just let your parents handle the forms, Amber."

★ ★ ★

"Lift those knees really high, OK?" Tammy yelled over the music. "Really put some muscle in it, guys!"

I felt a drop of sweat trickle into my ear. I glanced over at Marlene. Her face was redder than her tights.

"Guys in the back? Let's work it now!" I knew

Tammy meant Marlene and me. I wondered if sweat could collect in your lungs and drown you.

"I totally hate this," Marlene said between pants.

"How can something that's good for you feel so much like dying?" I huffed.

"It wouldn't be so bad if she'd turn the music down once in a while," Marlene said.

"Yes, it would," I said. "The only thing that would be less bad would be not having to do it at all."

"At least on swim team you don't get all sweaty like this."

"It isn't even the sweating that bothers me. It never bothers me." I struggled to heave my kneecap up to my chest. "*This* bothers me."

The stupid leotard. The loud music. Tammy yelling. I just hated it.

At the water break, Marlene stood so her back was to Tammy.

"How much do you really hate this?" she asked.

"A lot."

"Enough to lie?"

"Maybe," I said.

"Enough to do something about it?"

I did so want to do fun stuff. I did not want to just talk.

I nodded.

"OK." Marlene pulled my arm close and lowered her voice. "Here's what we do."

Nine

The easy part was falling on the floor.

"Help!" I yelled. "My leg! My leg!"

I grabbed my shin and pulled it in close to my chest and rolled around like something hurt. Dumb old Tammy was yelling and clapping and bouncing around so much that she didn't even notice.

"Tammy!" Marlene yelled over the music. She pointed to me on the floor. "Something's wrong with Abigail!"

"What?" Tammy cupped her hand to her ear. Then she saw me. "Oh, my!" she said. She stopped bouncing and turned off the tape player.

All the girls crowded around me. It was kind of embarrassing being the center of attention, but also exciting. I felt important. And it was such a relief, the music stopping.

Tammy knelt next to me. Her face looked worried. She looked more grownup, somehow.

"Where does it hurt, Abigail?" she asked.

"My leg!" I cried. "And here," I added, pointing to my chest. My heart did feel kind of funny, flopping around like a water balloon against my ribs. I wished everyone would back up

"What do you mean 'here'?" Tammy asked.

"My chest. It hurts a little." I looked at Marlene. "A lot, really."

"Don't move," Tammy said. She wasn't yelling anymore. She sounded serious. She put her hand gently on my leg. "Marlene," she said, twisting around, "go to the front desk. Tell them to call an ambulance."

"An ambulance!" Marlene looked at me.

My eyes met Marlene's. *Are you happy now?* I thought, hoping she could tell how irritated I was. *Is this your idea of fun?*

"Go!" Tammy yelled, in a way that was totally different from when she was yelling for us to keep our knees up.

"Tammy—" I started.

"Just lie still, Abigail. Take nice, slow breaths. Relax."

"No. Really. I feel better now." I half sat up. "I think I just need a drink of water or something. Or maybe just to sit for a while."

Tammy shook her head.

"Lie back down," she said. She sounded as though she was afraid I had really hurt myself.

"But—"

"Lie down."

"Maybe if she just sits on the bench—"

"Now, Marlene!"

Marlene gave me a funny look as she turned to run out to the desk. *I'm sorry!* she mouthed.

Tammy pulled the towel from around her neck, folded it over, and slipped it under my head.

"Just lie still," she said soothingly.

Now I really felt terrible. Tammy being nice to me was worse than Tammy yelling at me to work harder. I wished I hadn't lied, but I didn't know how to tell her the truth without feeling like a complete idiot. Getting thrown out of the class was one thing. Even getting yelled at by my mom. But looking like an idiot in front of twenty girls was something I hadn't counted on. I just couldn't make myself do it.

"Don't you worry about a thing, honey," Tammy whispered.

★ ★ ★

The paramedics came. They raced into the fitness room with a stretcher and black bags and stethoscopes banging against their belts. It was just like on TV.

They listened to my chest and moved my arms and legs and asked me if anything hurt. I wished something did. Then I wouldn't be in so much trouble. Plus I'd get to ride in the ambulance.

In the middle of all the commotion my mom showed up. Her face was sweaty, as if she'd been exercising, but gray and wrinkled up. I could tell she was worried.

"I was in the sauna when I heard," she said, bending over me. "Are you all right, honey?"

I nodded yes.

"I feel fine now," I said. "I keep trying to tell them."

"How is she?" Mom asked the paramedic with the stethoscope.

"We're checking her out," he said. From the tone of his voice, I could tell that I was going to be in bigger trouble than I'd ever been in before in my life.

⊞ ⊞ ⊞

"OK, Abigail, what's going on?"

Mom was standing with her arms folded across her waist. Her mouth was a tight little line, and the tip of her nose was bright red.

We were in the towel room. Tammy had told Mom we could have privacy there. I'd never seen so many towels in my life. It looked as if there were enough towels for everyone in the Bay Area to take a bath at once.

I sat on a slatted bench and swung my feet back and forth. My heel kept thumping against the wall behind me.

"Nothing. I said I felt better. No one paid any attention."

"Do you know how dangerous it is to call an ambulance when you don't need one?"

"Marlene called."

"Don't quibble with me, Abigail. When you

pretend to be sick or hurt, and someone calls an ambulance, that means those paramedics can't take care of people who really need help."

I stared at the floor. I'd never thought of that.

"What if someone was having a heart attack? Or choking? What if there hadn't been another ambulance crew to go out when it was really necessary?"

"I don't know," I said.

"Well, you'd better know next time." Mom pushed her hair back from her face. "You'd better think about this long and hard."

"I said I was sorry."

"As a matter of fact, you didn't. Also as a matter of fact, I don't care. What I do care about is why you did it."

I swung my feet harder. The wall made a comforting thump against my heel.

"I'm waiting," Mom said.

"Is Marlene getting in trouble, too?"

"That's not our business, Abigail."

It was quiet again. I didn't answer her. I couldn't. Not in a way she would understand.

Mom shook her head in exasperation. "You're not listening to me, Abigail."

But it seemed to me that Mom was the one who wasn't listening.

★ ★ ★

"Two weeks?" Marlene shrieked. "You're grounded for two whole weeks?"

"Except for the overnight. Mom wanted to say I couldn't go, but Dad said that was too much." I peeked over my shoulder just to make sure no one was in the kitchen listening to my conversation.

"I just have to empty all the wastebaskets and help with laundry," Marlene said. "What are you going to do around the house for two weeks? Can you have friends over?"

"No. And I can't ride my bike or talk on the phone for more than a minute or two."

"How come you're talking now?"

"She thinks you called about homework," I said.

"Speaking of homework, I found my Disneyland T-shirt."

"You're kidding."

"I snuck into Sandra's room and looked in all her drawers and under her bed. I finally found it stuffed inside a kangaroo pajama bag."

"You thought it was Sandra all along."

"Sandra still says no. She says she's being framed." Marlene laughed. "Mom says I get to pick three of Sandra's shirts and keep them, just to teach her a lesson. They all have cartoon stuff on them, though."

"At least you solved your mystery," I said. "I wonder if Mrs. Dooley gives you extra credit if you solve your mystery."

"Probably. Sherlock Holmes always solved his. Still no idea about Frances, huh?"

"None." I sighed. "I was thinking of talking to Grandma again. As long as I'm stuck at home."

"What more can she tell you?"

"Nothing, probably."

"Yeah. Hey, I gotta go. Mom says she wants forty socks folded by dinner." Marlene paused. "Sorry about this."

"It wasn't all your fault."

"It was my idea to try and get thrown out of junior aerobics."

"I should have thought it through," I said. "My mom says she'll have to beg Tammy to let me back in class."

"Maybe Tammy'll say no," Marlene said. "Your worries will all be over."

I nodded, even as I thought that Tammy saying yes or no wouldn't really solve a thing.

"Anyway," Marlene said, "I guess you *don't* always want to just talk."

Even in first grade, I was always the one who had to say I was sorry, take everything back. This was as close to apologizing as Marlene ever got.

"It *was* funny," I said.

"Poor Tammy. I felt sorry for her, the way her eyes bugged out of her head," Marlene said. "It was kind of mean."

We both laughed, even though the idea that something could be mean and funny at the same time made my heart beat fast.

"What are you doing, Grandma?"

"What's it look like I'm doing?"

I looked at the stacks of pots and pans, the glittery ground cover of spoons and forks and knives.

"Taking every single thing out of the kitchen drawers," I said.

Grandma nodded and leaned far into the cabinet under the sink. Then she pulled out a red wok and set it on the hardwood floor.

"Germs," she said. "You can't be too careful."

"Does Mom know you're doing this?" I asked.

"You can't be too careful about germs," Grandma said.

I watched her fumble in the cabinet for the coffeemaker and some unopened rolls of paper towels. She pulled everything out of the cabinet and placed it on the floor. A lot of the stuff did look pretty dusty. I couldn't remember Mom ever using that wok. Grandma didn't seem to care too much about cleaning, though.

"Why don't you help me?" Grandma said, leaning against the kitchen counter and breathing hard. "If you're so interested."

"I'm not interested. I just don't have anything else to do."

The last thing I felt like doing on a Wednesday afternoon was helping Grandma clean the kitchen. But she looked tired and hunched up and out of breath, and I felt sorry for her. I sat down on the floor and began putting forks back in the brown plastic tray that held them in the drawer.

Grandma put her hands on her hips and looked around the room as if it was a football field and she was trying to see from one end to the other.

"This place is a mess," she said.

"*Now* it is."

"Not like the way it used to be. Everything neatly stacked. Copper gleaming. Used to be you could eat off the floor."

I knew Grandma wasn't talking about *this* kitchen. You could never have eaten off the floor in our kitchen. Well, you *could* have, but it would have been pretty sickening. What kitchen was she talking about?

I wondered what it was like in Grandma's brain. What she thought about. What she saw. How it was that she could be looking at something—a stockpot, a measuring cup, *me*—and not really be seeing it. It suddenly made me sad. Grandma must be lonely. Not knowing who or what anything was must make you feel shaky inside, like being on a roller coaster where you were locked in the front car and the operator wouldn't let you off no matter how loudly you yelled. What was it like, not recognizing anything or anybody? Did you even know yourself? Not your name, but *you*, who you really were, inside?

"Hey, Grandma," I said, pushing myself off the floor. "I have something to show you."

The yearbook was on my desk, open to a picture of the junior varsity basketball squad. I grabbed it and ran back to the kitchen.

"What's this?" Grandma said as I handed her the book.

"Your high school yearbook," I said.

"What?"

I couldn't tell from her voice what she felt—whether she was mad or glad or just surprised.

"Well, not yours exactly. Uncle Stewart's. Aunt Betty sent it to me. But you're in it."

Grandma turned a few pages. Then she looked at me. Her eyes looked different. Not as though she really knew me. But as though she knew she didn't, and should.

"Where did you find this?" she said in a voice that was soft and almost pretty. "I've been looking for it everywhere."

I started to explain again, but I could tell she wasn't listening to what I said. She was slowly turning the pages of the book and running her crooked, spotted old finger over the pictures, gently, as if she was touching skin.

"Look," I said, pulling the book just slightly away from her. "You're on page thirty-six."

I found the page and handed her the book back.

"See, Grandma?" I pointed to her picture. "That's you. Right here."

"Well, of course that's me," she said. But she squinted close, as if she wasn't as sure as she sounded.

"I like that blouse," I said. "I'll bet Mom wishes I'd wear a blouse like that."

"We had to wear those blouses. School rules. See?" Grandma pointed to the rest of the page. "All the girls wore white serge blouses."

"Hey, Grandma," I said, pointing to the writing next to her picture, "what's 'Gee whillikers'?"

"What? Oh, that's an expression. I was always saying 'Gee whillikers.' It was old fashioned. I liked the way it sounded." Grandma smiled. "Miss Huber told me she'd pass me in bookkeeping if I'd just stop saying 'Gee whillikers' every time I didn't know the answer."

"What's bookkeeping?"

"The way we used to dread Miss Huber's class!" Grandma put her hands on her cheeks and shook her head. "But Papa told me it was for my own good. So I'd have something to fall back on, he always said. 'Don't you "Gee whillikers" me,' he always said when I gave him any guff." Her eyes were shiny, but she was smiling. "He meant well. He wanted the best for me. His best girl. That's what he called me."

I smiled, thinking how I wasn't the only one who had to hear about stuff being for my own good. I surprised myself by thinking that if I'd known Grandma when she was a kid, we'd probably have been friends.

"What's this?" I asked. "'Most Likely to Keep a Fella Guessing.' What's that mean?"

Grandma smiled shyly.

"I had lots of beaus," she said. "Once at a prom I danced with fourteen boys. I tried never to hurt a boy's feelings. If a boy asked me to dance, I always smiled and said thank you. Even if I didn't like him much. At the Winter Ball my junior year I danced all night with Alvin Fontaine. But I wouldn't let him hold my hand. You had to be careful about holding hands."

It was amazing. Grandma could remember dancing with fourteen boys over fifty years ago, but I bet that if I'd asked her what she'd had for lunch this afternoon, she wouldn't have had a clue.

I pointed back to the yearbook.

"It says here 'Bathing Beauties' under 'What She'll Remember.' What's that mean?"

"Well." Grandma sighed happily and looked up, as though she could see what she remembered about high school right on the ceiling. "Every year, after final exams, it was traditional for three girls to take a dip in the school fountain."

"You mean like a drinking fountain?"

"No, no. A regular water fountain. A large clay pool with a big jet of water bubbling up in the middle of it. It was right in the center of the courtyard. People threw pennies in it and made wishes. I always wished for a happy marriage and six children."

"You only had one."

"You don't always get everything you wish for." For a second Grandma's eyes squinted tight and her forehead wrinkled up. I thought she was going to stop talking, but then she took a breath and began again.

"Anyway, the three girls with the best grades on their exams were supposed to swim in the fountain at midnight on the night before graduation. Those three girls were the Bathing Beauties. It was a tremendous honor."

"Because of having good grades?"

"Yes, and because it meant you had been picked to do a very brave and challenging thing."

"What's so brave about going swimming at night?" I asked. I wondered if they even taught girls to swim fifty years ago.

"It wasn't the swimming." Grandma leaned close to me and lowered her voice. "If you were *really* brave, you were supposed to leave your bathing suit in the fountain."

"You mean swim *naked?*"

Grandma sat back with a smile on her face, happy she'd been able to shock me.

"Some of the boys spied on the fountain, hoping they'd see. But most boys weren't allowed to be cavorting around town at midnight on the night before graduation."

"Weren't you embarrassed?"

"If you chickened out at the last minute, you could just swim in your bathing suit."

"Or you could bring an extra bathing suit and just leave it in the fountain," I said.

Grandma frowned.

"That would be cheating," she said. "Bathing

Beauties wouldn't cheat. We were the best students."

"But you *could* have cheated."

Grandma shook her head.

"No," she said.

"So, Grandma," I said, "did you leave your bathing suit in the fountain?"

Grandma gave me a funny look.

"Do you think I'm chicken?" she asked.

She was joking with me. Grandma hadn't joked in months.

"No," I said.

Grandma nodded slowly, the smallest wisp of a smile on her lips.

"Darn right," she said.

Suddenly something hit me. "Was I there? I mean, Frances. Was Frances one of the Bathing Beauties?"

Grandma's whole expression changed.

"Certainly not!" she said.

"Why not? Didn't I have good grades?" I asked.

But it was as though a light had gone out, as though the memories had just evaporated, disappeared. Grandma shook her head and pushed the yearbook from her lap.

"There, indeed!" she muttered. "Certainly not!"

"Why not?" I asked again, but it was too late. Grandma was struggling to stand.

"You don't understand anything!" she said furiously.

"I'm sorry, Grandma," I said. "I didn't mean—"

"We were smart girls, nice girls," Grandma

said. She began walking toward the door. "Of course you weren't there," I heard her grumbling to herself.

★ ★ ★

"Everyone has turned in a permission slip and a medical-release form," Mrs. Dooley announced just before the final bell on Friday. "That means everyone can go on the upper-class overnight."

Philip Cassavetes raised his hand.

"Do we have to share a tent with girls?" he asked.

"Boys and girls will sleep in separate tents," Mrs. Dooley said. "And we'll be meeting up with the fifth graders only for breakfast, dinner, and the campfire on Saturday night. During the rest of the day, the fifth graders will be exploring an old-growth redwood forest. We will be taking a hike to the tide pools."

All the kids cheered. Connor Ring asked if there would be surfing. Everybody seemed to think that the fourth graders were getting a better deal out of this field trip than the fifth graders.

I raised my hand.

"Are all the fifth graders going?" I asked.

"Yes," Mrs. Dooley said.

"Do we have to ride the bus with them?"

"We're all going together, Abigail," Mrs. Dooley said. "The buses leave at eight A.M. sharp tomor-

row. Don't be late. We won't wait for stragglers."
She looked straight at me and smiled. "You may sit
with your friends, if you like."

I smiled back, even though I knew Mrs.
Dooley didn't understand, *couldn't* understand
how I felt. That I would rather cut off my arm
than breathe the same closed-up bus air as Travis
Mooney.

Ten

Dad dropped me off at school on Saturday at seven-thirty.

"Everything looks weird," I said as he pulled into the driveway. "I'm not used to seeing this place on a Saturday."

A lot of kids were already there: playing cards, singing campfire songs, trying to be the first to see the rented school buses lumber into the parking lot. I saw Marlene. She was sitting on her rolled-up sleeping bag. She had stuffed her hair up inside a floppy straw hat.

I didn't see Travis.

"All these kids are in the fourth grade?" Dad asked, braking to a stop.

"Fourth and fifth. It's the whole upper school. Two fourth grades and two fifth. I already told you." Dad was always needing to be told things over and over. He was too busy to remember after just once.

Dad released the trunk lock.

"Where's Mrs. Dooley?"

"There. That lady with the sunglasses."

"I would have given a lot to see my fourth-grade teacher in jeans and hiking boots," Dad said.

I thought about what Travis had said about seeing your teacher in a nightgown. I thought about telling Dad, but it might have made him ask me how Travis was doing and how come he hadn't seen him around lately. So I didn't say anything.

We got out of the car. Dad pulled my sleeping bag and my knapsack out of the trunk and set them on the pavement.

"Can I kiss you good-bye?" he asked.

It was a joke. We'd already discussed this.

"Just a hug. No kiss," I said.

He hugged me hard and snuck a kiss over my ear, where no one could see.

"Be smart. Don't go wandering off by yourself. Don't make friends with any bears," he said.

"There are no bears in the redwood forest," I said.

"Well, then, watch out for raccoons. They're vicious, I hear."

I pulled away.

"Don't eat too much junk. Mind Mrs. Dooley."

Why did grownups always have to mix up saying good-bye with giving advice?

"OK," I said, just to speed things along.

"No spying on the boys," Dad said, heading back to the driver's side door.

I waved once more, then turned and made

my way through the crowd of kids to Marlene.

"Mrs. Drooley confiscated my snacks," she said. "She asked me if I had any food in my knapsack, and when I said yes, she made me give it to her." Marlene folded her mouth in and gave Mrs. Dooley a dirty look. "All those licorice drops. All those peanut-butter chews."

"She told us not to bring food. She said food in the tents attracts wild animals," I said.

"I'll bet she takes everyone's snacks and eats them herself when no one's looking."

"She can't eat that stuff," I said. I rummaged in my knapsack and pulled out a tube of sun block. "Those peanut-butter chews would get stuck in her braces."

Just then I saw him. Travis was leaning against the chainlink fence that separated the walkway from the parking lot. He was wearing baggy jeans and an unbuttoned flannel shirt over a blue T-shirt. The flannel shirt came almost to his knees.

Without meaning to, I scanned the kids near him, looking for Tony Freites. I didn't see him, but there were plenty of fifth-grade boys around. They were punching each other and stealing each other's baseball caps and generally behaving like morons. A lot of fifth-grade girls were standing around, too. They weren't actually talking to the boys, but they were talking to each other in a way that made you think they wouldn't mind if the boys heard what they were saying.

Then Travis turned his head, and for a second

our eyes met. Just for a second. And I felt this hole in my stomach, as if mice had gnawed right through me: this emptiness where our friendship had been, where now there was nothing.

He didn't smile exactly. But he didn't *not* smile, either. He looked friendly, and interested, and curious, and sad. As though if I just went up to him and said, "How's it going?" he'd start telling me, as though nothing was wrong, as though nothing had ever been wrong. I almost did it, too. I was tempted. But then I thought of Grandma, and I turned my head.

★ ★ ★

Camp Taylor was three hours away by bus. We rolled down the unpaved gravel road just about eleven. The air smelled like dust and sap. Redwoods lined the road, their tops too high to see. When you looked up, all you saw was sunlight and leaves moving in a high breeze, shimmering like water.

"Do you think Tammy's missing us?" Marlene asked.

"Who cares?" I said, although I didn't really feel that way. Actually I felt bad about Tammy. She'd been worried about me when she thought I was hurt; she'd tried to take care of me. Every time I thought about lying to her, I cringed and shivered, as if I'd just run my fingernails across a blackboard.

"I wish there was a way to make it up to her, though," I said. "Without actually *taking* junior aerobics."

"I know," Marlene said. "Tammy's not so bad, probably."

The bus nosed in next to a wooden curb and creaked to a stop. Mrs. Dooley stood up and turned to face us.

"We've reserved four adjacent campsites," she announced. "You may pitch your tent anywhere so long as it is in one of these areas. Please don't pitch your tent too close to anyone else's."

"Shouldn't the girls be on one side and boys on the other?" Joe Christophe shouted out.

"That's not necessary, Joe. Your tents will provide you with plenty of privacy." Mrs. Dooley leaned down and surveyed the scene outside the bus windows. "Girls' and boys' restrooms are in the green buildings at either end of the outermost campsites. If you think you'll be paying a lot of nighttime visits to the bathroom, you may want to pitch your tent nearby."

Everybody laughed nervously. We couldn't wait to get off the bus.

"Everybody get busy," Mrs. Dooley called over the growing commotion. "If your tent partner is in the next bus, wait for him or her and decide together where to make camp. Remember, camping is an excellent way to practice group decision-making."

Marlene and I looked at each other and sighed.

"I knew she'd find some way to turn camping into school," Marlene said.

Putting up a tent with Marlene was so easy that it felt as though we'd done something wrong.

"Are you sure we hammered in every stake?" Marlene asked.

"Every one," I said. "Did you put up the rain flaps? I hate sleeping with the rain flaps down."

"I know. Everybody's breathing makes the inside of the tent all wet," Marlene said. "I like to see the stars at night."

"Me, too," I said happily. Marlene and I didn't need practice in group decision-making. It just came naturally for us.

Marlene unrolled her sleeping bag, then sat back on her knees and looked around. "There's tons of room in here."

Just then we heard Mrs. Dooley's whistle.

"Let's everybody meet over by the campfire pit," she called.

The campfire pit was a short walk from our tent. We had to cross a rickety wood-and-chain-link bridge that spanned a dry creek bed to get to it. The pit was round, with stone ledges cut into the dirt to sit on. Down below, at the center of the pit, was a mound of ash and gray, burned wood. We took seats near the top of the pit. I stretched out my legs and watched the sun make dancing shadows on them.

"I like it here," I said. "The way it smells. Piney."

"Not like room freshener, though," Marlene said. "The real thing."

As the kids filed in, Mrs. Dooley and the other teachers stood at the center of the pit and chatted. They all wore jeans and sunglasses. Miss Cox wore a pink hat. If you didn't know they were teachers, you'd think they were just regular ladies: a bird-watching club, maybe, or moms at the park.

I scanned the stone seats and saw Travis sitting on the other side of the circle, a few rows down. He was with a group of fifth-grade boys. Tony Freites was sitting on his right. He was gulping big mouthfuls of air and making himself burp. Some fifth-grade girls sat on the seats above them. Whenever Tony burped, they laughed loudly and clapped their hands over their mouths, as though they'd never heard a burp before in their lives.

When most of the kids had settled down, Mrs. Dooley blew her whistle. There was no reason to blow it, but I could tell that she liked doing it. The other teachers had obviously decided that she should be in charge.

"Welcome to Camp Taylor," she said.

All the kids clapped and hooted.

Mrs. Dooley went over all the rules. She hoped we knew how to behave, but she told us all the rules anyway. They were mostly the same rules as we had at school, but she added some new ones, like not picking any wildflowers or peeing outside.

"The staff at Camp Taylor has made a box lunch for each of you," she said. "We'll walk over to the cafeteria together and pick them up. Once we have our lunches, we'll split into fourth- and fifth-grade groups. We'll meet up again later for dinner."

Tony Freites punched Travis on the shoulder. Travis was smiling a little, but he shoved Tony away. I could tell he was trying to pay attention.

"Keep together," Mrs. Dooley was saying. "When we have to walk along the road, please stay as close to the left side as possible. Watch for poison oak. And bring your backpacks! You'll need them to carry your lunch."

We walked single file. At first there was a lot of talking and laughing. Some fifth-grade girls who were wearing black nail polish were singing "Michael, Row the Boat Ashore," but they stopped when no boys would join in. Pretty soon, you couldn't hear much of anything except the chatter of squirrels and the slap of our shoes in the dirt. Sometimes goose bumps would prick up on my arms. I'd look up at the road and see the shadows of leaves shaking in pale patches of sun and know that high up a breeze was blowing.

At the cafeteria, three short, fat ladies in green ranger uniforms and hats handed out our box lunches.

"What'd we get?" Marlene asked, opening her box and sniffing.

"Turkey and cheese on rye, carrot and celery

sticks, two chocolate chip cookies, and fruit punch," I said, digging in my box.

If Mom had packed me a lunch like that, I would have complained about not liking Swiss cheese and how there should have been four cookies instead of two. At camp, though, everything looked good.

Outside the cafeteria, Miss Cox and Miss Alvarez led the fifth graders off down a trail marked Redwood Flats. Mrs. Dooley and Mrs. Pinkney, who wore sandals with socks and beaded jewelry and who my mother always said looked like something the cat dragged in, marched the fourth graders across the road and down a gravel path that seemed to lead nowhere. At the end of the path, a wooden sign read, Tide Pools, 2.5 miles.

The hike was easy: mostly downhill through open fields and small dense thickets of redwoods. It was warm, but not summer-hot: the air beneath the trees was just cool enough to make me wish I'd brought a sweater, so that when we left the trees behind, the meadowy-smelling sunshine felt good on my arms and face.

Mostly we didn't talk. Mrs. Dooley asked us things, like how we would write 2.5 as a fraction and whether a sea urchin was an animal or a plant. She said the tide pools would have lots of sea urchins. I skipped along, feeling excited inside, hoping I'd be the first to smell the ocean, glad I'd remembered to bring my colored pencils and my sketchbook in my backpack. Mrs. Dooley had said there'd be time to draw what we found.

The tide pools were on a stretch of beach that ran under a high grassy cliff. Ocean waves crashed into the low flat rocks that hugged the shore, then foamed away into nothing. Between the rocks, hermit crabs scurried for shelter. Sea anemones' tentacles waved in the water like purple kite tails. If you looked carefully, Mrs. Dooley said, you might even see an octopus that had washed in with the tide.

I loved the tide pools. I forgot about everything except finding more creatures, and the smell of salt in the sea air, and the feel of spray in the wind. I practically ran from rock to rock, trying to see everything at once.

"Be careful, Abigail! The rocks are slippery," Mrs. Dooley warned.

"What's all this black stuff?" I asked.

"What does it look like?" she asked.

"Like shells," I said. "Hundreds and hundreds of shells."

"That's right," Mrs. Dooley said. "You're standing right in the middle of a huge mussel bed. See how strong the shells are? Even when you stand on them, they don't break."

She was right. I moved off to the side and found a stretch of bare rock anyway. I didn't want to take a chance on squishing any mussels.

Mrs. Dooley bent down and pointed to something that looked more like clay or rock than anything alive.

"Who remembers what this is?" she asked.

"I know," I said without even raising my hand. It seemed stupid to raise your hand outside. "It's a chiton. It's got tucked-in shells."

"Calcareous plates," Mrs. Dooley said. "A chiton is a kind of mollusk."

"Like clams!" Joe Christophe said.

"Very good, Joe," Mrs. Dooley said. "What distinguishes mollusks from other kinds of animals?"

"They're squishy," Marlene said.

"What would be a more scientific way of saying that?" Mrs. Dooley asked.

"They have no backbones," I said.

"Does anyone remember the term for animals without backbones?" Mrs. Dooley asked.

No one did.

"Invertebrates," Mrs. Dooley finally said. She had to shout to be heard over the crash and hiss of the waves.

We ate our lunches on tall flat rocks that were just right for climbing. I watched some of the kids race each other to the top, but I didn't climb myself. I nibbled on celery sticks and thought about the animals swarming beneath the sea foam: strange as movie monsters, but real—hunting for empty shells, luring prey by pretending to be rocks and flowers. *Invertebrates,* I thought. I would remember that an invertebrate had no backbone until the day I died.

"I hate the way everything you eat at the beach tastes like sand," Marlene said.

"Is there a job where you get to look at tide pools?" I asked.

"Probably. Remember the rangers?"

"I wonder what rangers do," I said.

"Clean up trash. Tell kids not to litter. Make box lunches," Marlene said.

"Hmm," I said. Maybe being a ranger wasn't for me. But there had to be some job for people interested in sea life.

Life. The study of life. Biology. Frances.

It was the first time in days that I hadn't thought about Frances for more than an hour. I'd hardly even missed her.

Frances had liked biology. Maybe Frances had loved the sea. What a funny coincidence *that* would have been.

★ ★ ★

Back at camp, we were free to do nothing until dinner.

"Just like at home," Mrs. Dooley said, "only no TV."

"Saturday's when I watch *The Three Stooges*," Philip Cassavetes said.

"Camp Taylor affords other opportunities," Mrs. Dooley said. "You'll have to muddle through without *The Three Stooges*."

My legs ached from so much hiking, and I felt the beginnings of a blister on my little toe, but I didn't care. I grabbed my sketch pad and colored

pencils from my knapsack and scootched backward out of the tent.

"Come play poker with Amber and Yvonne
and me," Marlene said. "We're going to collect
acorns and use them to bet."

"No, thanks," I said. "There's something else I
have to do."

The air smelled like sun and tree sap, like an
afternoon with nothing to do. No one noticed as
I skipped along the path to the bridge, then
scrambled down the creek bank. It was cool
there, and thick with ferns. I had a feeling the
creek bed was where the frogs were in the summer. October was late for frogs.

It was hard to decide what to draw first. To
warm up, I sketched a fern. Then I drew a frog. It
was tricky, because I didn't have a real one to
copy from. I forced myself to remember the nub-
bly skin, greeny black, somehow dry and oily all
at once. I liked how my drawing came out.

Then I drew chitons and anemones and crabs
in different shells. And rocks and corals and sand
dollars and eels. And plain old fish in all the colors I could think of.

I tried drawing water. That was hard. Real water
wasn't blue. It was clear or muddy brownish green.
Finally I had to settle for wavy lines that made the
fish *look* as if they were underwater.

I was concentrating so hard that I didn't even
hear his footsteps. He must have made a lot of
noise, tramping down the bank.

"What're you doing?" he asked.

My heart thumped even before I looked up.

"You scared me," I said.

"Sorry."

"Your voice," I said. "It's so quiet down here."

Travis nodded.

"So what're you doing?" He leaned forward, trying to see. "Drawing?"

"Yeah." I looked back at my pad. I didn't try to cover it up. "A shark."

"You didn't see sharks at the tide pools, did you?"

"No. I just felt like drawing one."

Travis lowered himself into a crouch.

"That's pretty good," he said. "How'd you learn to do that?"

"I don't know," I said. I felt proud. "I've never actually drawn a shark before."

"Wow." Travis half smiled. "That's really good, then."

"Thanks."

"So—" Travis wrung his hands together, as if he was washing them without soap. "How do you even know what a shark looks like?"

"Well, I don't, exactly. I mean, I picture one in my head. And it comes out, I guess. Maybe not perfectly. But if I think about each part of the shark—each section—and draw it the way I picture it—" I paused. "I don't know. It just comes out."

"Man. I could never do that," Travis said. He shook his head.

I didn't remember Travis ever saying "Man" before. It sounded like something Tony Freites said.

"Yes, you could," I said. "If you just tried."

"No, I couldn't. Trying wouldn't help," Travis said. "I'd try and try and try and I still wouldn't be able to do it."

I almost said, *Yes, you would. Anyone can do something if he tries.* But then I remembered how I felt in junior aerobics. How I felt when Mom said that if I'd try it, I'd like it. No matter how much I tried, I'd never like junior aerobics.

"It's probably because you're just more interested in other things," I said. "Basketball and stuff."

We used to like the same things: computer games, cartoons on Saturday mornings, talking in the hammock. Was that what had happened to us? We had started liking different things?

"I guess," Travis said. "But I like art. I wish I was good at it."

"You can't be good at everything, I guess," I said.

"That's what Sister Steven said last year."

"Sister Steven?" I laughed.

"My fourth-grade art teacher."

"How come she's got a boy's name?"

"Lots of the sisters at St. Francis Prep had boys' names," Travis said.

For a split second, the world came to a screeching halt. Not a movement, not a sound. Travis and I were the only people in the world. Not even a fly was buzzing.

"Travis," I said, "who is St. Francis?"

"Just a saint," he said. "He fed the birds. He loved animals."

I swallowed.

"He?"

Travis nodded. And then he smiled. He knew exactly what I was thinking.

⭐ ⭐ ⭐

Dinner was roast turkey and mashed potatoes and green beans and vanilla ice cream. Everything except the ice cream was disgusting. I was sure those green beans had come out of a can.

After dinner everyone headed out to the campfire pit. The sun was almost down, and it was getting cold. The sky was liquid inky blue, like finger paint, and full of the beginnings of stars. Even before the rangers lit the fire, the air smelled smoky.

Mrs. Dooley and Miss Cox passed around bags of marshmallows. I hate marshmallows, except at night, in front of a fire. Marlene held three in her lips and two in front of her eyes. She looked spooky in the dancing firelight. Also like a dog carrying too many tennis balls in its mouth. I laughed my head off.

A tall man in brown shorts and a tucked-in blue shirt stood in front of the fire.

"I'm Ranger Mike," he said. "Guess what my last name is?"

A few kids raised their hands. Ranger Mike's last name wasn't Smith, Johnson, Brown, or Schwartz.

"Give up?" Ranger Mike asked. "It's Danger." He waited while we all figured out why this was funny. "Ranger Danger. I swear. Really. It's the truth. Just ask the other rangers."

We laughed a little, the way you do when you can't decide whether you're laughing at somebody because he's funny or because he's stupid.

"So you can call me Ranger Danger," Ranger Danger said.

Philip Cassavetes raised his hand.

"Did you decide to be a ranger just so you could say that?" he asked.

Ranger Danger laughed. "Nope. I became a ranger because I love being outdoors. I wanted to spend my life helping people understand how important it is to protect the environment."

"What's your middle name?" Philip asked.

"Joel."

"Can we call you Ranger Joel?"

"No," Ranger Danger said.

I liked this. Ranger Danger might be goofy, but he still had rules. You had to respect a guy with rules, even if he was wearing black socks.

"How many of you love sitting around a campfire?" Ranger Danger asked.

Lots of kids clapped. A few yelled "Yeah."

"Campfires make me want to sing songs," Ranger Danger said. "Who knows a good campfire song?"

Angela Peterson suggested "Kumbaya, My Lord." A fifth-grade girl liked "Let the Circle Be Unbroken." Shanna Hoversten picked "Who Threw the Overalls in Mrs. Murphy's Chowder?" They all sounded different than when we sang them in music with Mrs. Pereira: clear and sweetly in tune. Maybe it was being outside.

After we'd finished singing, Ranger Danger said, "Another good thing to do around the campfire is tell scary stories. Anybody know any scary stories?"

No one did, so Ranger Danger told a couple. My favorite was the one about the beautiful lady whose head fell off when her husband untied the ribbon around her neck.

"Campfires make some people want to tell stories and some people want to sit quietly," Ranger Danger said. "Some people just like to stare into the fire. How many colors do you see?"

I counted five. I didn't feel like raising my hand, though. Staring into the fire was making me sleepy. I liked the sounds it made—snaps and hisses—and the smell of burning pine needles and the way pieces of newspaper turned orange at the edges, then crinkled into nothing.

"Anybody have anything you'd like to share?" Ranger Danger asked. "Something fascinating you saw today? Something you think the group would find interesting?"

Haley Hall told about how she had dropped a hermit crab into a sea anemone's mouth. A fifth-grade boy named David Haas told about a section of a redwood tree that had been mounted at the park's entrance. Each ring of the tree was equal to a single year. There were over five hundred rings. The tree had begun to grow around the time that Columbus had sailed for India.

"I thought that was totally amazing," David said.

"Not as amazing as my toenail," Philip Cassavetes said.

Everybody laughed.

"What's this about a toenail?" Ranger Danger asked.

Philip began pulling off his shoe.

"Here," he said, "I'll show you."

After everyone had seen Philip's toenail, Ranger Danger asked, "Anyone else?" He walked around the campfire to make sure he was getting to everybody. I saw him stop and point at someone on one of the upper stone tiers.

"I just wanted to tell someone I'm sorry," Travis said.

I couldn't see him. He was directly on the other side of the fire from me. But I knew his voice. I'd know it anywhere.

"Campfires are a good place to do that," Ranger Danger said.

"I did a really dumb thing," Travis said.

"What'd you do?" Ranger Danger asked softly.

"I don't want to say." Long pause. "You do dumb things when you're desperate."

"Sure you do," Ranger Danger said.

Everyone was silent. I felt as if even the trees were breathing and had stopped, waiting for what he would say next.

"Anyway," Travis said, "I'm really, really sorry."

"Is this person sitting with us right now? Does he know who he is?" Ranger Danger asked.

"I'm new," Travis said. "This person was my best friend for almost my whole life."

"Oh, well." Ranger Danger sounded relieved. "I'll just bet that if you call this person up when you get home tomorrow, he'll understand how you feel. We all make mistakes."

"Phantom was my best friend," Travis said.

I smiled in the flickery darkness.

"Phantom will understand," Ranger Danger said.

⊡ ⊡ ⊡

Later, in the tent, Marlene and I lay in our sleeping bags and looked up at the stars.

"He was talking about you, wasn't he?" she said.

"Who?"

"Gooney Mooney. Travis."

"Yes," I said.

I waited, but she didn't laugh.

"Is he your best friend?" she asked.

The stars winked in the blackness. Some were sharp and bright. Others you could barely see.

"I don't know anymore," I said.

Some stars were so faint that you could only see them if you didn't look directly at them.

"You're *my* best friend," Marlene said.

"Thanks," I said. I didn't know what to say next. I didn't want to lie. "I love playing games at your house. Doing things." I paused. "You have great ideas."

"I'm not good at just sitting around," Marlene said.

She meant talking.

I took a deep breath.

"It hurt my feelings, the way he laughed at me," I said. "In front of everyone."

Marlene rustled around in her sleeping bag. She couldn't think of what to say, how to make me feel better.

Travis would have known. The old Travis.

"When Deirdre hurts my feelings, I lock her in the downstairs closet until she says she's sorry," Marlene said.

At least she didn't laugh.

All around, the stars winked like eyes that saw everything.

Eleven

"How was it?" Mom asked.

"Good," I said. "Can we go right home?"

"I just need to stop at the drugstore."

"Can't you do that later?"

"For heaven's sake, Abigail," Mom said. "Were you that homesick?"

"I wasn't homesick at all," I said. "I just want to go home."

"The drugstore will only take five minutes," Mom said.

It seemed to take forever. Mom bought toothpaste and deodorant and wrinkle cream and gift-wrap. Then we got stuck at every red light between the drugstore and Red Valley Drive.

Donald and Travis were pulling into their driveway just as Mom and I pulled into ours.

"Hi, Donald," Mom said as she closed the car door.

"Berniece. Abigail." Donald was wearing a

baseball cap backward and was growing a beard. The baseball cap was so you'd know that Donald knew what kids thought was cool.

"How'd you like camp?" Mom asked Travis.

"It was good. Nice," Travis said. He looked at me, then quickly back at Mom.

"How about you, Abigail?" Donald said. "I'll bet it was a real learning experience, huh?"

"I loved it," I said. "I loved everything about it."

This made everyone smile. Even Travis.

"These kids sure are growing up," Donald said.

Guidance counselors were always saying things that made you wish you were somewhere else.

While he and Mom were talking about Mrs. Krasner down the street, whose teenager had loud parties, I sidled over to Travis.

"You want to come in for a minute?" I asked.

Travis looked up.

"Sure," he said.

We headed across the driveway to the front walk.

"Hey, Trav," Donald said. "Where you going?"

"I gotta help Abigail look something up," Travis said.

★ ★ ★

It took us only a couple of minutes to find it.

"'Francis X. McDermott,'" I read. "'Going stir-crazy'; 'Hold your horses!' Heroes: President Roosevelt, Joe Louis. Biology Club, Debating

Society. Favorite Song: 'Donkey Serenade.' Favorite Activity: 'Driving the teachers nuts!' What the Future Holds: Graduate school; 'Being a teacher somewhere—preferably someplace without kids like me!'

"How'd I miss him before?" I asked, shaking my head.

"You thought he was a she," Travis said. "You just assumed that because *you're* a girl, so was Francis."

"Now it makes sense why Grandma got so upset when I asked if Francis was a Bathing Beauty," I said.

"What's a Bathing Beauty?"

I explained.

Travis laughed.

"No wonder. She thought you meant that she would have gone swimming naked in front of Francis," he said.

"I wonder why Grandma thinks I'm Francis," I said. I looked right at Travis. "Do I look like a boy?"

It surprised me how hard I hoped he wouldn't say yes.

"No." Travis looked hard at Francis's picture. "But he's skinny and has red hair, it looks like. Maybe that's what gets your grandma confused."

"Maybe," I said

"I wonder whatever happened to Francis," Travis said. "I wonder if he ended up being a teacher."

"I know how to find out," I said.

★

123

★

"I figured out Francis," I said.

"Good for you," Aunt Betty said. "I knew you would. Who was she?"

"Not she. He. Francis X. McDermott. Francis with an *i*, not an *e*."

"Well, I'll be darned. Frankie McDermott. He was a friend of both Lucille's and Stewart's," Aunt Betty said. "No wonder I didn't know who you were talking about. We all called him Frankie. Only your grandma called him Francis, come to think of it."

"So they were friends?"

"Oh, my, yes!" Aunt Betty laughed. "Frankie was a good scout. The kind of boy everybody liked. He wasn't much of an athlete, as I recall. Kind of gangly. All hands and feet. But everybody loved him."

"Were they boyfriend and girlfriend?" I asked.

"Oh, no. Your grandmother was a tremendous flirt in those days. Quite a tease. Frankie was a shy fellow with the girls. Never could dance worth a darn. He was the kind of boy—" Aunt Betty paused. "He was the kind of boy you could talk to. He was loyal. He was funny. I hate when young people nowadays say, 'Oh, he's just a friend.' Like a friend's easy to be, or nothing at all." Another pause. "Frankie was a good friend. And that was important."

Hey, I thought. *I'm loyal. I'm funny.* Is that

why I reminded Grandma of Francis? I hoped so. It made me feel that even if Grandma didn't know my real name, she knew me. Who I was inside. Maybe better than a lot of people.

"What happened to Francis?" I asked. For some reason, my heart was beating fast.

"Oh, dear." Aunt Betty took a deep breath. I could tell she was gearing up for bad news. "He died in the war."

"Oh." It seemed I'd known all along that Francis was dead.

"It was the saddest thing," Aunt Betty said. "I don't recall what branch of the service he was in. He just wasn't the sort of boy who was cut out for the military. He was a practical joker, a wise apple. Being told what to do just didn't sit well with him."

"Hmm," I said. Another reason I reminded Grandma of Francis.

"Not that anyone's suited to war," Aunt Betty said. "Those were terrible times. Taft lost a lot of its young men. Most high schools did. People always took it very hard. But after a while, it stopped hitting you in the same way. It's an awful thing to say, but . . . you just lost count."

I tried to picture Joe Christophe and Philip Cassavetes in uniforms, aiming real guns, not just sticks. I looked at Travis, who was helping himself to an orange at the kitchen counter. Would Travis talk back if a drill sergeant yelled at him? Would he close his eyes before he pulled the trigger? Would he be afraid?

"I can't even imagine a real war," I said.

"Good. That's the way it ought to be," Aunt Betty said. "Back then, we just prayed for it to be over."

We were both quiet a moment, Aunt Betty remembering, me thinking.

"It must have been horrible for Grandma. Francis dying," I said.

"Oh, I imagine so," Aunt Betty said. "They were terrible times. And you grieved, but not too much. You had to be strong. You had to believe that there was meaning, a purpose to all this suffering. So you kept a lid on what you felt. Not like today, when perfect strangers tell you their troubles on the bus." Aunt Betty sniffed.

I thought of Donald, who liked to get in touch with feelings, and smiled.

"I'm sure Lucille felt Frankie's death quite deeply," Aunt Betty said. "I imagine it's eaten at her all these years."

After a minute, I said, "Thanks for telling me all this stuff."

"Oh, my pleasure, dear," Aunt Betty said. "It must feel good, knowing who Francis is, after all this time."

"I guess," I said.

Actually, it didn't feel as good as I'd thought it would. And it wasn't because Francis was dead, even though I was sorry that he was.

It was more because figuring out Frances, finally, didn't help me figure out much of anything at all.

★ ★ ★

"At least you know," Travis said. "You solved the mystery. That's something."

"Yeah. I guess so."

"It's funny that everyone called him Frankie except for her," Travis said.

"Not so funny," I said. "I never call you Trav."

He smiled, looking embarrassed.

"I bet you get the best grade in the class," he said. He sounded proud of me, and I smiled, too.

At the front door, I said, "Thanks for helping."

"What help? You did everything."

"You gave me the idea about Francis being a boy."

"I should have thought of that a long time ago. From being at St. Francis Prep."

"I didn't think carefully. It's one of my worst qualities," I said.

Travis nodded at the floor.

"My worst quality," he said, "is wanting the cool kids to like me."

"Everybody wants to be liked," I said.

"Not enough to do really crummy things," Travis said.

We were quiet a minute.

"If we hang out at school, Tony'll hate me," Travis said.

My stomach shriveled up.

"I know," I said.

I knew what he wanted me to say. That it was all right. That I understood.

"I can't pretend not to be friends at school," I said. "I just can't do it."

Travis nodded. Still not looking up.

"I don't know if I can hang out," he said. "I'd like to. I *wish* I could."

You could, I thought. *Just do it. Just try.*

"I'm not brave enough," he said. "The other guys wouldn't understand."

That's your worst quality, I thought.

"You're still my best friend," he whispered.

A best friend wouldn't care about the other guys. He'd be loyal. No matter what.

"We can still be friends on weekends," Travis said. He looked up from his shoes. "I can still come over and help you baby-sit Grandma."

"Yeah," I said. "That would be OK."

Travis nodded, relieved.

"It'll be almost like before," he said.

I nodded, too. There was no point arguing. Even though I knew how wrong he was.

★ ★ ★

Mrs. Dooley thought my mystery was very cool. She liked how I used good thinking to solve it. "Solving the mystery isn't really the important thing," she said. "It's more important to think creatively than to come up with the right answer."

The really exciting mystery was Marlene's. Sandra had been telling the truth. She'd never taken Marlene's T-shirt, just as she'd said.

"I was sure that Sandra had taken my shirt," Marlene said. "But it didn't really make any sense. Sandra doesn't even like Disneyland. She throws up on all the rides. Plus, that shirt would have been small on her. And she likes big shirts."

"Excellent reasoning, Marlene," Mrs. Dooley said.

"And then, there was a funny stain on the shirt. I knew it was chocolate. And Sandra's allergic to chocolate," Marlene said. "It had to be Deirdre."

"You certainly have a lot of sisters," Mrs. Dooley said.

"Five. And Deirdre is sneaky. She knew I would blame Sandra, especially if I found the shirt in Sandra's room," Marlene said. "But she finally confessed. After I interrogated her."

"Not too roughly, I hope?" Mrs. Dooley asked.

"Just until she told the truth," Marlene said proudly. "She's only five. She's pretty easy to scare. You don't even have to really do anything to her."

"This just goes to show you," Mrs. Dooley said, "that facts can be misleading. Things may look one way and be entirely another. Don't believe anything you haven't proved to yourself."

Everyone looked impressed. Even Philip Cassavetes, who usually looked as though he didn't even know what day it was.

Marlene raised her hand.

"And don't go around saying you didn't take a T-shirt when it's splattered all over with your favorite flavor ice cream," she said.

Mrs. Dooley smiled.

"Excellent advice," she said.

★ ★ ★

"Do you think I'm funny?" I asked.

Grandma was staring at the TV. I wasn't even sure she heard me until she said, "Hilarious."

"Really?"

She nodded, not looking away from the news.

"Everything out of your mouth tickles me," she said.

I sat forward on the couch, leaning toward her.

"What else am I?"

Grandma squinted, still not looking at me.

"What?"

"What else about me, Grandma? What else am I?"

I held my breath, waiting.

"Oh, not just funny. A nice person. A good person. Lovely." She turned her head, reached out, and laid her hand on my hair. She looked at me. Really looked at me. "A beautiful girl."

"Oh, Grandma," I said.

She turned back to the television. I could tell that the moment was over.

"Just look in a mirror," she said, recrossing her legs and getting comfortable. "It's plain as day."

★ ★ ★

"Can I talk to you?" I asked.

Mom looked up from the newspaper.

"Sure, Abigail," she said. "What's up?"

I sat down on the couch. Straight and tall, though: not all floppy, like usual. I wanted her to know this was serious.

"It's about junior aerobics," I said.

Mom sighed and crumpled the paper in a sloppy fold on her lap.

"I've already talked to Tammy," she said. "What am I supposed to say? 'Never mind, Abigail's changed her mind about aerobics'?"

"It isn't that I changed my mind," I said. I'd felt the same way all along.

"I loved camp," I said. "Did I tell you that?"

Mom's eyes got softer.

"Yes, you did," she said.

"I loved the tide pools. All the animals. I found twelve hermit crabs. They look like space monsters, the way they pull themselves along the sand with their claws. Their bodies all stuffed up inside their shells."

Mom nodded.

"Mrs. Dooley says there are people called marine biologists who study animals in the oceans," I said. "I think I might want to be one of those when I grow up. Either that or a painter who paints pictures of the sea. Who draws pictures of sea creatures for books, even."

"That's nice, honey."

"I don't have a best friend anymore," I blurted out.

I wanted her to know. Maybe I didn't tell her enough stuff. Maybe if I told her things, she'd understand me. Really see me.

"What?"

"I still like Travis. And Marlene. And other kids, too: Amber and Yvonne and Shanna and Haley. But everything's changing. Everything's different."

"But—"

"*I* don't laugh at people's secrets, though. *I* don't like someone only when other people aren't around."

Mom looked at me hard. I thought she was going to argue with me, but she just pushed the paper onto the coffee table and leaned forward, her elbows on her thighs.

"I paid for eight classes," she said. "Do you think that's fair? That I paid for eight classes, and you've only taken three?"

You shouldn't have paid without asking me, I thought. *You should have asked me first.*

"I'll ride my bike for an hour every day," I said. "I'll jog a mile around the playground during P.E. Even if Mrs. Dooley says we can walk when we get tired, I'll jog the whole time."

Mom was quiet, thinking.

"How about if you finish this session of junior aerobics," she said, "and I never ask you to take it again?"

It wasn't much, but it was something. Something was better than nothing.

"Can I wear sweatpants instead of a leotard?" I asked.

"How about pink sweatpants?" Mom asked.

Hadn't Grandma said to be true to myself? But what if people didn't want to hear what was true?

"I hate pink sweatpants," I said.

"What I wouldn't give to wear pink," Mom said. "But it's not a good color on me. It makes me look dowdy."

"What's 'dowdy'?"

"Old and fat."

I looked down at my lap.

"I don't know what pink makes me look like," I said. "A big bunny, maybe." Pause. "I hate looking like a bunny."

Mom smiled a crooked, half-sad smile. "It's hard, trying to figure you out, you know."

"It is?"

"Yes, it is," Mom said. "It takes a lot out of me."

Wow!

It wasn't going to be easy. Mom would always want to see me in pink. And I would always hate it.

Figuring out Frances was the easy part. Francis was gone—a ghost from Grandma's past—and in a weird way, that made figuring him out a lot easier.

Figuring out other people—people who were still around: not knowing things, changing their minds, making mistakes—was a whole lot harder.

"Pink sweatpants wouldn't kill me, I guess,"
I said.

Mom smiled, a huge, happy smile.

I wondered if you ever really figured anyone out.
Even yourself. Did you ever really know everything
about yourself that there was to know?

Probably not.

It was like doing a puzzle, though. Putting all
the pieces together was the fun part.

"There's a beginning ice-skating class at the
rink," Mom was saying. "Maybe you'd like to try
that."

"Maybe," I said. "Just don't buy me pink skates."

Skating might be OK. I'd never tried it, but it
sounded fun. I liked trying new things.

One of my good qualities.

"I can just see you," Mom said. "Whizzing by."

I half closed my eyes. I could almost see it, too.